ALL THE LAND

BY

SHERRIE DEMORROW

Published 2018 by

Lightning Source (UK) Ltd
Chapter House,
Pitfield,
Kiln Farm,
Milton Keynes
MK11 3LW,
UK

Cover Art Design by Sam Wall

To LL for help and support

In acknowledgement of SC, DJ and DMC

To the memories of PAU, LH, PS, ML, NW, LN, DW, SB and especially AC,

who continues to inspire my work

PREFACE

Please note **this is a book of fiction** and **NOT** meant as an accurate representation of historical events. The reader must suspend all preconceptions of belief in past history. There may be some reality in detail to it, but most of the scenarios are FAKE.

The historical attitudes towards sensitive issues, and people's prejudices of the time, had to remain intact to provide a sense of realism in the story.

Some place names given are **NOT** real, unless otherwise stated or recognised as real. Other characters (for the most part) are fictional and loosely based on people known of by the author.

Part I

William Phillip De Hastings

AD 1060s

Chapter I

Sur-Le-Merde was a town on the Northern coast of France, which, despite its name, I found to be lovely, elegant and popular with tourists (when in season). The name of the town means 'on the crap', which a previous ancestor of mine had used to refer to the farm he started about a hundred years prior. The name stuck, and for awhile, people rarely came by. When the farm used better methods for pig handling and sanitary issues, a community had formed and thrived here. The farm provided the inhabitants with fresh quality meat and soon its reputation had spread. Demand for good meat was high, mostly for the upper classes, but we always made provisions to help the poorer ones too. *We did not want anyone starving, you know.*

The air, though pungent with the endless pig waste, still smelt reasonably, if one went closer toward the sea. There were those who went there, mostly rich folk like me, to spend time away for a bit. They got together in nearby taverns and drunk themselves silly, discussing things from women, religion and what respective trades they were in charge of. Serf-teasing was most common, as many an anecdote was passed between aristocratic lips, as well as endless whinging about the lazy ones.

I, William Phillip, lived on my own land, a nobleman of the de Hastings line. I was rich by my trade, though I never got my fingers dirty doing it... *I, however, was willing to assist those who did not mind the dirt!* The people around me usually would refer to me as *mon Seigneur*, but I was certain they called me otherwise behind my back. I knew not to bear it in mind, for my fore mind was kept to the pigging farm. The family motto was *Tout L'Estate*, meaning 'all the land or estate'. I knew I was secure in *my* estate and my land was free for the pigs, and lower classes, under me, to roam. I practically owned Sur-Le-Merde and I made others know it too, by building my moated castle.

I was about six foot in stature, with sandy brown hair (tinged with red), blue eyes and fair of face. I remained a bachelor, too, for the farming came first. There were plenty of ladies to go 'round with and I confess, I had my fair share of them. *None of them struck my fancy.* Maybe I was too practical and shrewd, just as I am with the pigs.

A neighbouring district, Hanlette, lay close by. A distant cousin on my mother's side lived there called Sir Aolfe (pronounced 'Alf') Sans-Brys. We were not very close, but we made fond acquaintance. A knighted soldier, he was always on campaign fighting somebody else's battle. He also had a loving family, who patiently waited for their lord to return. Aolfe was a tall fellow, with classically chiselled looks and had cut a fine cloth of his own in the clothes he wore.

I oversaw my pig farming trade, with many vassals and serfs working under me. They, and the animals they tended, were all looked after well. It was good for the business and my business was to provide meat for the District I was lord over. However, the least enjoyable aspect of the trade was the selling of the living to prepare the way for the many dishes their former bodies would create. I hated the killing, especially of the younger pigs. Yet my sort, and those higher, loved the little sucklings on the banquet tables, some of which I attended (and even attended to, in some cases). *Such show offs*, I reckoned. I do confess I enjoyed seeing my Handiwork gazed upon with appreciation, especially as my pig farm was the Best in the District. *And I planned greedily to keep it that way.*

The animals, being well cared for, were husbanded by a team of at least fifty to one hundred workers. I kept a food bin in the castle, where I would put any food scraps I could not finish. The scraps would then be collected and added to the pig's feed. I also bought local grain to add to the mix to ensure the animals' health and that the product was at top quality.

I have spent years and years lording over the farm and we since had become like a family; *my real family were a different breed of sorts altogether!* I guess it was compensation for not having one's own, but I was an odd one and did not give into class pressure to find a woman. Unfortunately, illness was rife along the coastline and with the latest addition of foreigners, disease had spread through the district. About a third of the population had perished in the latest outbreak, the saddest part being my family counted among the dead. I was the last link of the de Hastings line, though there might have been others around; *one never knows.* So, it was up to me to keep the breed going and I really had to consider the match to be one of advantage, as well as of health.

The best part of it was I did not have to give in to pressure here. There was a great freedom of choice and plenty to choose from. Although I survived the disease brought in by the foreigners, I detested them, and I certainly would not mix with them. I also saw them as a threat to my business, as some had so-called *dietary* laws and traditions... most of which I could never understand. Thankfully, my misgivings were not unfounded, as others in my station had thought the same, but, I praised God there were not many of them. I certainly would not deign to entertain them, as they were not of my rank. *I further noted they smelled rank too!*

The days wore on for all the workers, and I noted one who'd been with me for the past ten years. His name was Lannau and he retained his position shovelling sty muck. He looked tired after a good sun-up sun-down day but he was a strong one. I cherished those who showed valour in strength... *if he were of a better class, he'd make a good Knight.*

I called out, 'How goes it, Lan?'

'Messy, my lord, just finishing off. I was wondering if we could share a drink at *Les Trois Cloches*.'

I pondered for a bit... *Les Trois Cloches... The Three Bells*. The local myth of the area was that a spirit had been bestowed with a collar of three-bells that chimed nightly. The nocturnal chimes conveniently told the hour of the clock, some thought, but in reality, the spirit was a small cat looking for its food. Still, it was a good watering house name. I liked it. I would let the workers out for a night's tipple, certainly... *not that I would be joining them, of course.*

'You may have leave for a few hours before you take up your beds and do not forget, you are responsible for any meals thereof,' I commanded.

'Yes, my lord,' Lannau agreed and went to tell the others of my recent generous offer to them.

I returned to my Castle when I was given an invite to *Les Trois Cloches* after all. I was very flattered by it, and since I had naught else to do that evening, I joined with Lannau and a few of the staff.

We walked to the tavern and ordered our drinks. As I sat at the table, I noted my cousin, Aolfe was sitting nearby, reading.

I walked up to him blithely and greeted him.

He responded, 'Ah, William, how are you?'

'Good. Good. No battles, I take it?'

'Nope. I'm on leave at the moment, visiting my family. They are all getting on. Have you found someone amongst your pigs yet?'

I laughed at that comment, though inside, I felt embarrassed. '*Personne*,' I lamented.

'*D'accord*,' Aolfe soothed, 'You'll get someone. Perhaps you will get one across the sea. I hear the Duke of Normandy is planning an invasion and I am going. Will you, dear cousin, attend? You can accompany me and you never know, the natives might be *restless*.' He chuckled at the thought.

I recalled that on a clear day, one could make out a white block of something in the far distance. Was it Scandinavian Ice? Was it another Country? I consulted a map in my library (well, I am a Lord, after all!), and realised it was Angleterre (England), as the writing boldly stared back at me on the parchment. I looked upon it with a greedy eye, wondering if I could further my trade and move the herd to a new pasture, or perhaps to secure a new one. I, for one, was itching for a new pasture.

Despite my ancestral love for Sur-Le-Merde, I found there were changes as an influx of immigrants from the East came by, who, incidentally, were not necessarily on a reverse Crusade. Personally, I felt they had no right here and sorely wished they'd return to their Own. Yet, with a surge of people moving West, I reckoned I would be just like them and move across the water... to Angleterre. So, I should not talk, as I may be in their shoes someday. I wondered how they, across the water, live, love, work and, I guessed, they spoke a hybrid language they liked to refer to as English (as many peoples had invaded there in the past). News about other places may travel fast with the influx of the immigrants, but unless it was about pigs, 'twas no concern of mine.

In light of my musing, I spoke. 'Aolfe, it would be an honour to join you.'

He smiled at me, 'Good. We will be in touch. I know where to find you... I'll just follow my nose.' He got up and he shook my hand.

'Yea, I will be waiting,' I sighed. *I could hardly wait.* I found him to be just a bit *too* eager for adventure. Personally, I was the *settle-ye-down-marrying* type, but I had not found my mate yet. I brooded terribly about this. I walked over to the table where Lannau and the rest sat and joined them.

'You look troubled, Will,' Lannau commented.

'I just ran into my cousin, Sans-Brys.'

'Ooh, not someone to mess with,' he said.

We pondered the thought and continued with our drinks.

* * * * * *

I had an opportunity to accompany the excursion across the Channel to the small country of *Angleterre...* England. *Well, compared to France, it was small!* A Duke in the area of Normandy, by the name of William, was itching for a day out. He also felt he was deserving of the English throne through a promise made by a previous King called Edward the Confessor. A landing party was arranged to sail to the neighbouring Land. We hoped to get out around midsummer, but soon, harsh winds had taken course and prevented our outing until late September. (*What a pity!*)

The ship was sturdy enough and the crossing, rather treacherous in choppy waters. Before I left, I instructed my friend, Lannau, to carry on with the farm in Sur-Le-Merde. I still owned it, if only from afar. I've known him for years and I trusted him.

I firmly believed he would prove a worthy asset to me and to the farm... *yet, I knew I needed to move on.*

When we reached England, we disembarked the ship, one among a few others which arrived with mine. We encamped nearby and heard word from His Grace, William of Normandy, to remain. The enemy, meanwhile, were engaged in the North, dealing with a Viking invasion by another contender to the English Crown, Hardrada. So, we bided our time, violently familiarised ourselves with the new land, and prepared for the confrontation with the Saxon King Harold and possibly that Viking fellow.

I reflected in my tent with a small prayer book by my side. I cannot say it was a leisure trip, for much of us noblemen were in fighting armour. Yet, I envisioned us winning and scaling the landscape with our stamp of overwhelming edifices of castles and churches, as well as a clean and tidy system of government which would organise this strange Saxon hoard. In my contemplation, I dreamed of a book of some sort that displayed possessions and rights of land, to what and to whom... *a Domesday list, perchance!* I laughed it off, but put the idea in the forefront of mind, for when I see the good Duke again.

CHAPTER II

It was several weeks since our landing. I shared the tent with a fellow shipmate, Comte Hebert du Cleuxnz (pronounced 'Kloonz'). Together, we went on a series of manoeuvres and raids in the area. I felt comfortable with his familiarity and during a quiet spell, we shared concerns.

du Cleuxnz remarked, 'I heard that Hardrada had fallen in the North and the Saxons are heading our way.'

'You nervous?'

'Well, we did not come here for a holiday,' he retorted.

No, I suppose not. 'You got a woman, Hebert?'

'Yep, got a wife and six children back home. God knows if I will ever see them again. Hey, maybe if we win this, perhaps the Duke will let me bring them over, yea?'

'Not a bad idea... 'twould be more Normans with us,' I laughed.

'It would,' he paused, 'You got someone in France?'

'Just a pig farm. I've got a close workman seeing to it. If I am lucky, maybe I can start something here as well.'

'Well, there looks to me there's plenty of land for the grabbing... all the land could be ours!'

All the land... the family motto I feverishly clung to. I never thought it would be put to good use or irony, in this case.

By mid-October, we were met by the Saxon army of King Harold.

He mostly had infantry (made up of unskilled peasantry) and house carls (who were nothing more than bodyguards to the great and by this time, low in number from the previous conflict up North). We Normans, on the other hand, had infantry, cavalry, and archers. Our armies were similar in size and it would take much doing to sort ourselves out. The place where we sorted ourselves out was in an area called Hastings, originally called Haestingas, after a local Anglo-Saxon tribe. However, word got round that Harold was coming after us in due haste and not waiting for anything. *More irony?* He thought he treat us like he did the Viking forces and get us by surprise.

The enemy forces gathered, defensively, near a hill not too far from Hastings; their infantry and house carls, at the ready, with woodlands and marsh surrounding them. Our diverse forces formed by their geographical location stood opposite. I stood amongst the cavalry lines; my friend du Cleuxnz was among the archers. They unleashed many arrows upon the Saxons (which impacted upon their shields rather than the men), then our infantry charged toward them. The enemy's shield 'wall' was just screaming to be crushed. We then reached the main lines and fought the enemy directly. Quite a few on both sides had perished. Soon enough, it would be my turn to enter the battle as my fellow cavalrymen charged. *The battle wore on for hours,* it seemed. Even the good Duke had his horse killed twice! (*And I assumed they were different horses.*)

This unfortunately led to a rumour (which on a battlefield such as this one, would be easy to spread), that William himself was killed in battle. Some of our men retreated, which was worrisome indeed, but it could have been a ruse to fool the Saxons into following us. The part of the enemy's army that did follow us were surrounded by our men and defeated... as were the remaining forces nearby.

It was a weary all-day struggle for the Anglo-Saxons, who eventually lost the day. Word had spread that King Harold had died from an arrow wound in his eye (*ugh!*) It made me scared inside. A proper, anointed King was deposed. *What if that happened to us?*

I've never experienced this before and hoped that His Grace, William, would command in due fairness. Of course, I jest, because I knew that he was cunning, ruthless and shrewd. He wanted to take over all of England, uniting all seven Saxon kingdoms into one large country to pursue his administrative ideals.

I told the *former* Duke (now the King) about my idea of the Domesday list; (*he decided to call it a book*), where he can chart everything gained in battle and tax accordingly. As a thank you, he gave me the small counties of Woolanshire and Dumfushire to lord over. I was most chuffed and told him I planned to continue my pig farming trade there.

'You may do so. There are plenty of peasants to use in those counties. They'd be grateful for the work,' His Majesty said to me, 'I wish you good fortune in your pursuits.'

I blushed, totally in awe of the kindness of our new Royal. I later found out the counties were rich in soil and perfect for my trade. I decided to set up in Dumfushire, taking over from a now defeated Saxon lord called Wilfin Aelcyn. This lord referred to the peasants here as 'dumb fucks' and this name, used for the county, remained (although changed for decency, of course).

The bordering county of Woolanshire, (also once owned by Aelcyn), was named for a sheep farmer called Wooland, but the final letter of the name was dropped from mispronunciation. *These Saxons had some very odd traditions, indeed!* I so yearned to set up my home here, within these counties, but to do so, I really needed a wife. *I was not getting any younger!*

Since I planned to live in this new land and take advantage of what the King had offered me, I chose to stay. My friend Lannau can see to the business back home and I really did not have anything that I had not brought with me already. I may be a Lord as such, but I did live pretty spartan. To blend in, I decided to drop the 'de' from my surname and now known as William Phillip Hastings.

Even though we were the Conquerors of the nation, I felt assimilation would ease our advantage over the natives. I really wanted to renew myself and begin a new life... to do what I do best, *just somewhere else...*

* * * * * *

Within the borders of Woolanshire, I helped set up the local monastery, in addition to the pig farm I had in Dumfushire. St. Gillacott was made up of a handful of Cluniac monks, whose order originated in Cluny, France. They came over with us during the Conquest, but did not join in the fighting. Basing a *stricter* way of life on the teachings of St. Benedict, their days were taken up in constant worship and occasional study, writing and work. *However, they found worship more appealing.*

It was firmly believed that the endless prayers of the monks would aid in one's salvation and would be answered accordingly. (And with so many petitions to God, He would have no choice but to satiate these *nag-me-per-hour* prayers... *He can only take so much,* I figured.) So, I threw money into this project and it took off, from a small number of the original six (from the Conquest days) to nearly over a hundred. The gardens surrounding the main building were kept in check by some of the monks as well as potential initiates.

I later built a dwelling at the site of the farm in Dumfushire, to oversee the farmers. It was similar to the one I had in France and I called it 'Hastings Court'. Although it was *my* home, I allowed it to be used as the home of the on-site peasant staff; (*I just had a room all to myself!*) It seemed smug of me to do so, but it came in useful as a dwelling. As I remained single, *I did not care who I bunked up with!*

However, over a few weeks time, I found it was extremely uncomfortable and needed to get away from the hassle... *and the endless odeurs de porc et merde.* And, with the many tenant farmers living in Hastings Court, *it was also no place to woo a lady, either!* I later moved from the farm to Woolanshire, to a plot bordering the nearby common of Wilset Green. I remembered my family motto, (*Tout L'Estate*), thought of a new home, and anglicised it to *Totteringstate.* There was a small village which grew up around Totteringstate, and the village itself was christened the same.

Here, the air smelt much fresher and I found it a fit spot to build my new home, away from the pig farm. It began as a small cottage for one man. A large space was my room, kitchen and unfortunately, latrine (*this, I needed to sort*). I had a small fireplace built and posted a spit over the enhancement so I could continue my foul French habits good living entitled me to. The house was not large by any means, but I had since befriended a local carpenter called Buckingham. With his mates, Cateliffe and Nay-Smith, he helped build makeshift furniture for me. They knocked out a bed, night table, dining table, some chairs, a dresser and later, I obtained a decent set of crockery to provide me with the good meals I was accustomed to (and to what my pigs provided).

Of course, I sold on our pigs, once ready for processing. I had the meats brought back to sell in the markets, whilst bagging a few parcels for myself.

I also sold the meat to the tavern in Dumfushire, *The Incensed Rose*. The meat came in handy there, (for the more splendid affairs the villagers had), *and of course, the income did, too, for me...*

I instilled the practices I followed in France and everyone around me cooperated. They knew I was part of the Conquest, but I was not His Majesty, William I. I treated those lower orders with fairness, politeness and good meals that came with the farming. I was happy to work with them and a little kindness did go a long way. However, all that kindness could only take one so far... *I sorely needed a wife.*

CHAPTER III

Months later, I was enjoying my new home, Totteringstate Hall, when Fate brought somebody most fair unto me. Her name was Elthia Aelcyn, and at last, my heart raced to find her. Daughter of the Saxon lord, Wilfin Aelcyn, who originally owned the counties I now possessed, Elthia was a bashful, young, native maid, descended from Conquerors of yore. Her known Roman, Viking and Saxon lines provided much variation to intermingle with my French lineage. *This could prove advantageous.* She was a firm faced lass, blonde hair, brown eyes, a low forehead covered by a small wispy fringe, with nice lips and a smile to dazzle. I could not wait to kiss her, as she looked so good to me. *Ah, what was I to do? I was just a lord in love.* She had not minded, and was extremely flattered by my pursuit of her.

I was very keen on Elthia, who was waiting on a basket of seasonal fruit at the local market when I chanced upon her. A quick meander 'round to see how my sales were doing had changed my life forever at that point...

Despite my noble background, I felt like a washed up nothing at the far end of space, gazing upon the flavoured object of my affection. I threw myself away in contempt, as I approached to speak to her on that fateful day.

However, she began the conversation...

'How goeth it, my lord, or are you a Lord?'

Did she address me as my lord? I quickly glanced at my apparel... I did not wear my best finery, though I was allowed to wear as I pleased... it was doubtful I was dressed suitably. When one owned a pig farm and checked up on it everyday, one does not want to look *too* fine.

'I am a lord, my dear girl,' I replied. I shuddered inside, *as if life suddenly became a rave-up against a brick wall.*

'You don't look like one,' she mocked, teasing me.

'I am William Phillip Hastings, Lord of Dumfushire and Woolanshire, at your service.'

'And I am Elthia Aelcyn,' she paused, intensely staring into my eyes, 'So, you are the new Lord who took over my father's lands??!'

'Your fa--,' I stuttered and hesitated, realising that I believed I stepped into a pile of pig poos. She gave me a look that could spark a war if provoked... *and I think I provoked her... oh God!*

'Yes, my father, Wilfin Aelcyn, the lord who ruled Dumfushire and Woolanshire, and gave the name to the former county out of contempt toward the local peasantry.'

'My Lady, alas, 'twas by no means did I come over to offend. I was marked out for the King's attention and rightly awarded those lands for my services to him.'

'You Normans, cavorting in your debonair way,' she moaned, continuing her stare that caused my skin to alight, 'You think you've conquered us Saxons, well, think again!' She harrumphed and gave me the biggest pout I'd ever seen on a woman.

I tried to explain, 'Look, Thia, I came over for a better life and a better way.'

'So what do we have that France doesn't? Huh? I doubt you left behind a shit-filled pitiful hovel.'

'Well, I did leave behind a shit-filled farm, but my estate was certainly not a hovel.'

'Did you retain your estate in France?'

'I have someone looking after it in my stead.'

'Where's it at?'

'It is located on the coastal region of Northern France, called Sur-Le-Merde.'

'That sounds like a right state,' she laughed, as if I were a jester.

'Duke William of Normandy had given us an opportunity to change our lives and I took it.'

'More like *he* took it.'

'He took what?'

'Our throne and now, you lot rule over us. You know, we had a decent peaceful life and just finally settled down since the last Viking raids and now you come along and spoil things.'

'My sweet girl, oh, please don't be cross with me. With the newly acquired lands I gained, I hope to make use of it for the benefit of all.'

'How?' Her look never wavered toward me.

'Pig farming.'

'So, *you're* that pig farmer of Totteringstate... word gets round, you know. It is a privilege for a daughter of a displaced landlord. Father still likes to keep tabs on his former properties.'

'Indeed and rightly so,' I stated proudly, 'and I am that pig farmer of Totteringstate. I am not an actual farmer, but I do lord over my workers.'

'You're planning to supply the counties with fresh meats?' *Still inquisitive was she.*

'That is my intention and to give to the poor, if we meet with good harvest.'

'You've many workers?'

Was this a friendly chat or an interrogation? 'I have a few on site, hopefully to become a growing concern.'

Elthia thought about it. I was hoping she would come on board, too. My earlier plan to assimilate with the locals seemed to go well here... eventually to bear good healthy fruit in the long run.

She looked at me again, but her countenance was remorseful, 'Forgive me if I probed too deeply into your affairs. I wanted to know more about you and apologise if I caused you offence. Your arrival was so sudden... your Conquest, so intimidating. Suddenly, Father had no lands to speak of. It is an odd quirk of Fate that I would meet the man who displaced him.' She scowled a bit then.

'As I told you before, the lands were granted to me by the Duke, who is now our King. We must follow his rule. We could do this together, or hate each other for the rest of our living days.

'I really do not want to do that. You are an intriguing figure, young, plucky and quite intelligent. When one conquers, one must not be divided... we must all be as one, one nation under William.'

'And what of the lesser classes, hmmm?'

What a cheek! 'Well, they would have to work on the pig farm or other lands, won't they?'

My face beamed with a smile and she laughed, hugging me. She nearly forgot about the fruit she had previously waited on when the stall holder had called out to her to collect. I took the basket from the seller and paid him the due fee.

'You didn't have to do that,' she whinged.

'Oh, are we still playing stubborn Saxon wench?'

She stuck out her tongue at me then giggled, taking the basket from me. 'I guess I will have to get this home for Father. He has ailments and the doctor had prescribed some fruit to alleviate the condition.'

I durst not think of what that condition could be and refused it to be conversed upon.

I did not think the market day would have been better than that. We parted company, at that point, in the best of terms and I went on my way to my stall to see to my business.

We continually met at the local market square and I decided to court her more seriously. I got to meet her family, what was left of it, many of them dying of some illness or other. Wilfin was the only survivor of the Aelcyns... *so much for a large family, then.*

Despite Wilfin's grumbling and moaning about my land takeover, he was impressed once he saw what Elthia and I had done with his old lands.

'At least we won't starve,' she commented.

'That's the idea,' I assured.

* * * * * *

As our time progressed its course, Elthia became the love of my life. We decided to partake our marital vows in front of Totteringstate Parish Church. We stood at the door, at each end, with Elthia's father, Wilfin, and my fellow Conqueror, Hebert du Cleuxnz, as witnesses. The dowry needn't have been discussed, for I was in charge of Wilfin's lands now. That was enough for me, *and very convenient too.* A priest was called in to officiate, though not really necessary. *However, as I was the new Lord of the Manor, so to speak, I felt it needed that seal of officialdom.*

The ceremony was short and sweet, with an 'I do' regarded in earnest on both sides.

Once concluded, Totteringstate was awash with celebration. The villagers paid their respects to me with felicitations and congratulations. Elthia looked very pleased with herself, as she bagged her Lord and shown much smugness about her. She will be a fine entity to be content with and had made *my* Conquest complete. I had hoped other comrades of my day found love amongst the localised wenches in their respective parts.

That night, however, I embarked on a more glorious conquest of my own, with accompanying feast:

Besotted with your love, I take leave of my senses.
The carnal pursuit bestows us the fruits of love, not unnatural.
Tickling the soul of your conscience,
The seed comes in to multiply.
You procured the season of my pleasure,
As you grabb'd my handle of deepest treasure.
Then you ride your own horse upon my lands,
And I moan with relief, with thee.

Of course, our religion would never let us partake our fruits so lightly or gently, for their view upon the matter was most harsh indeed. *Yet, us folk knew better and we firmly believed there was absolutely nothing wrong with it.*

Later on, my dearest extended our little breed with a son, Aelebrett and a year later, Roger John. Both were strong; both made for the manor. I called upon my many workers to lay a feast for each occasion and invited the village to the fete, just like my family once did back at Sur-Le-Merde.

The children grew fast, cunning and with that happy sparkle of life that comes upon youthful occasion. I was most pleased and Elthia felt contentment, reassured of the whole thing. Even her ailing father was less anxious, as he enjoyed the company of grandchildren.

* * * * * *

It was the late 1090s and I've established myself in the new lands I was given by the King, William I. Like in France, the people here were more than happy to work with me and I treated them fairly, according to my status.

The children had grown up, but our family was limited to just myself, Elthia and the two children Aelebrett and Roger. We tried for other children, but without success. Our two boys proved themselves quite worthy and I let them take over when I went on leave, for personal reasons.

Word got 'round about a Crusade being assembled in the outlaying area; the destination, Eastward toward the Holy Land. *Now, why would they want to do a thing like that*, I wondered. I had been a soldier for much of my life, but I was happier as a settled family man, and Lord of the lands of Woolanshire and Dumfushire. I felt Christendom was quite sure in itself; *it had no need to convince others of its power over man.*

Apparently, the story was that the head of Byzantium needed help with a local conflict, where people were colonising his lands (*unauthorised*), and needed assistance. It later turned into a violent feud between two worlds, West and East, fighting over the fate and ruling of the Holy Land.

The Pope at that time, who needed an excuse to go to war due to non-Christian influence in the East, had a perfect reason now for doing so. He eagerly recruited everyone from everywhere to assist and awarded indulgences for those deciding to join. It was also an excellent opportunity to unite the Christian faith since the East-West schism of 1054. Those who were knights, as well as the odd soldier of Christendom, heeded the call and happily joined up. I decided to go, despite my misgivings. The Comte du Cleuxnz, too, was wary of the situation.

'My lord, William, if we go, what good will it do, once we arrive?' He was sorrowful in his questioning.

'I don't know, it sounds like obsessive, bloodthirsty call to me,' I retorted.

'It seems futile to me, I mean, this marching East?!'

'Phah!' I spat on the ground at the thought.

du Cleuxnz silently agreed. Elthia came into the room with a knowing look in her eyes.

"Tis the Lord's calling,' she said, then walked out.

There was a pause. *Heavens, she was right. It was a calling... a High Calling; but, to what end?* To capture the Holy City away from the non-Christian... *but, who were we to judge?*

du Cleuxnz and I decided we could not debate this further and realised we had to go, as faithful Christians. Our lands were still being worked on; our estates, well secure.

Many men from Totteringstate were assembled with volunteers, anxious for forgiveness; knights, who were there for the brawn and the occasional sin purge. Others were told of the religious duty a Crusade would entail, with the benefits of a purge of their personal sins and burdens...

...not that I had many, you understand...

As soldiers, we refreshed our training, as it had been some time since we last saw action. A fellow called Jeanne Jazin had come into our fold to supervise and lead this crazy expedition.

In a few weeks time, we set off. We boarded a barge, with supplies and many mounts, to take us to the Continent, where we would then march through, heading Eastward, for thousands of miles. The better of us rode on the mounts, myself included, whilst the others purged their feet into the cruellest earth. The journey was arduous, tiring and (to me), pitifully unnecessary.

The soldier's feet blistered inside boots of many hues of red, yet they kept going; with Hebert du Cleuxnz riding besides me, I kept my spirit upward on the mount. I prayed every night and every day and through each agonising step of the horse. *My bottom was getting sore and I hoped something would come to the fore and rescue me from this madness.*

I stayed with the Company; we made camp near a river called the Rhine, in a country that boasted such green, natural beauty which reminded me of my adopted country of England. I started to feel faint when du Cleuxnz upheld me and gave me some water.

'Thanks, mate,' I stirred.

Hebert looked concerned, 'You still unsure of yourself?'

'Well, no, erm, yes. What do I know? I am doing this for Our Lord and naught else!' *A snap shown in the personality.*

'We discussed this earlier, William, and we agreed to do this. You think on Our Lord and He will get you through this.'

I later passed the time thinking about it and kept my strength for as long as I could. We carried on with the journey and a couple of weeks or so later, we reached the long Desert... My horse gave way to weakness and collapsed. I fell into the sand; *suddenly, I could not hold out much longer and lapsed into nothingness...*

CHAPTER IV

The dragon flew over Vominos, hovering above the melee as the Crusaders looted and pillaged the town. Once a great seat of culture, a gang of revolutionaries set against their norm and allied with the Crusaders. This flying creature, known as a Bondigon called Derwint, swept waves of hot air which singed the palm trees. Bondigons were a breed of dragon which had the ability to turn human when a monthly need of nature called. Their monthly copulational was so great that it would kill them, if unsuccessful in finding someone to bond with. This applied to male and female Bondigons alike, and Derwint was no exception.

Derwint looked sadly upon the townsfolk, who were running in all directions, gasping for life as they knew it. He then gazed upon an unusually beautiful girl, called Digenyrus Ackmhen. She looked like a princess, he thought to himself, as he noted she was tall, good solid frame, comely features, oval face, and looked quite out of place with fiery golden hair (the like that is rarely seen in this part of the world). She prided herself on that massive flame she wore, and for one to see her, one would need eye-defenders to deaden the intense glare.

The Bondigon moved toward her. Her beauty captivated him, and unfortunately for him, it was that time of the month. He pondered, she must be a throw-back... maybe if I could... I will, have to have... her. It did not matter who the Bondigon used for the month; the instinct was growing stronger and the matter needed to be quenched quickly. Something had to be done.

He kept staring at her from a distance in the market square, as people ran around her. No one paid much attention... no one does when one runs for one's life. The invading army had gone after anyone and anything, but for some reason, they left Digenyrus alone. Did they know about the Bondigon's monthly habits?

Still, she was Derwint's target when the urges took over. He practically lost it... I have... to... must... bond... with her.

With a loud cry, he transformed into his human form, as he fell to the ground. As a human, Derwint looked the part and no one really noticed his lack of being... what's it to them, another naked man, anyway? There were plenty of them about. He stood up and found some fabric laying about on the ground... probably discarded from the fleeing inhabitants. He clothed himself appropriately and still remained a handsome devil... well, he did not feel that he was one, but considering what his true nature was...

An old lady waddled past Derwint, and was concerned. 'You look lost, young man. Is there anything I can help you with?'

'No thank you, but cheers for the kindness,' Derwint quickly replied and scanned the area for his target to exploit into submission.

Yet, now, he was on a mission of his own making. He passed a reflective glass shard on a building and saw his human look. Quite satisfying!

He hadn't gone too far to find this month's affection when he saw her stood by an alcove, away from the running crowds. He was astounded at his luck and she thought he was a dish onto himself. Digenyrus's parents were killed during the exodus from Vominos and she was now alone... to face the Bondigon. She was well of age, roughly about twenty years old, and could happily look after herself. In fact, she had secured her own flat, away from her family, and struck out on her own... had a job at a market stall as a salesperson... before the Invasion. Derwint moved toward her, true to his task, and tapped her tanned shoulder.

'Let me take you somewhere safe,' he said.

'We'll go to my place,' she responded, grabbing his hand and leading him down an alley where her flat was.

They walked up the stairs, inside to a modest room... a room which looks as though it had just been moved into. There was no hesitation when Derwint found a bed in the same room. It was now or never, and never was not an option.

Digenyrus asked hospitably, 'Is there anything you want?'

The answer could not have come at a better time. Derwint pulled her down onto the bed, and stated simply, 'What do you think, my dear, eh? Give us a kiss, I won't make any trouble.'

'Why is that?'

'Cos my life depends on't,' came the grave reply.

They wilfully struggled in place together, when suddenly, he trooped his colour upon her.

'You slay my honour, sir,' Digenyrus cried.

Derwint felt an involuntary ejection and soon, another release was on the way... A tingling sensation happened within his upper body. Could it be a sneeze, or... oh what do those humans call it... a cough, belch?

The Bondigon let go the newer release, as a huge flame burst onto the bed. He instinctively jumped off, leaving Digenyrus, not realising what happened until it was too late.

Derwint moaned, 'Damn, I did not mean to set you alight. Why does this always happen to me?'

The girl did not answer, for the bed was consumed by dragon fire. The fire lit a small corner of a curtain and it got out of control. Derwint tried to get a bucket of water, housed nearby, to smother the fire he (unfortunately) caused. Some of the fire was quenched, but the damage was done. He began to search for a window from where he can make his exit. Discreetly, he climbed out, breathing a sigh of relief. He transformed into his natural dragon form and flew away.

At least, no one saw him.

* * * * * *

I came 'round from the reverie and found it hard to focus. The searing clothes I wore had absolutely burned into me. The desert sun was well above the horizon. My group was progressing along at a snail's pace, our metallic footwear reflecting further torment upon our persons.

My dear friend du Cleuxnz had found me languishing and stared down at me.

'Are you alright, my Lord?'

'I should be,' I replied, as I struggled to my feet. I wobbled a bit, finding it difficult to maintain myself with all the gear put upon me.

du Cleuxnz helped me to what was left of his ration, but I could not think to deprive my friend his bit and declined the offer.

'But you must eat...dear William, you cannot terminate your life now,' he exclaimed.

'You eat, leave me.. I..,' there was a further struggle in my voice, as it got worse.

The heat of the gruelling sun, where we were, had taken its toll on me. Our company had neared the East, but had not quite made it yet... *and it was very apparent that I will not, either.*

I began to shiver and sweat, with the linen lining, chain mail armour, and some woolly bits around my person. My body was suffocating profusely, and there as no escape from it.

I reached out to my friend, in my dying breath, 'Totteringstate...'

du Cleuxnz responded, 'My Lord?'

'Totteringstate, please bury me at Totteringstate...,' I gasped, and impaled my soul on Death's spearhead.

I felt a small release and passed into permanent unconsciousness.

du Cleuxnz had been gutted; he sobbed and reported to his superior, Jazin.

'Lord Hastings had just expired, sir,' he cried.

Jazin asked, 'Where is he?'

du Cleuxnz directed him over to the body. Flies already have gathered for their feast.

'No, this will not do. We will have to leave him, I'm afraid,' Jazin concluded, and walked away in his resolution to continue the journey.

Already unsettled by the death of his friend Lord William Hastings, du Cleuxnz was not resigned to cheat him of his final wish. He gathered up his deceased friend, and held him for awhile, until...

... the Bondigon arrived.

This was no longer a hallucination. The dragon flew high above in the sky and had caught sight of the two men, one of them not looking very well from *his* perspective.

'You, there!'

du Cleuxnz looked up to see who called out. He saw the most frightening vision he'd ever seen on this side of the world. It was a huge reptilian creature with airbags filled with heat, releasing into the air. One of gigantic proportion, it had a scaly blue and violet colour to it... with huge yellow eyes to match... similar to those of a snake. As a soldier, du Cleuxnz was used to the extreme, and now, he was seeing something rather *extraordinary.*

'May I be of service?'

The human was perplexed... this cannot be... *a talking dragon...* and then he realised, *the Bondigon!* He remained dumbfounded.

'Aye, I am talking to you, hu-man!' The Bondigon was getting impatient with the man's confusion, 'What is the matter, you've never seen a dragon before?'

'Not one that talks. Usually one gets burned before a conversation.'

'I can arrange that!'

'Wait, what do they call you?'

'Call me Derwint. Are you in need? You look like it and your companion is rather wanting.'

du Cleuxnz had no choice but to put his faith in this... *dragon*. 'My friend had just died. He needs to be returned home to Totteringstate for eternal rest.'

Derwint contemplated. 'Totteringstate?'

'Yes, Totteringstate. It is a vast estate in Woolanshire, England. Know you of it?'

'I think so. I'm a bit of a world traveller, myself. Would this person be the Lord Hastings of Totteringstate, who runs the pig farm, formerly de Hastings, of Sur-Le-Merde, France?'

'Yes, I did not think a dragon would know, or care of, such trivialities.'

'It sounds like knowing a triviality could mend your situation. I do have a consideration for you, if you care to hear.'

'Anything would help. I am in a bit of a fix, and my company's already ahead a few miles by now.'

'Well, without artificial power, you may not have a chance to catch up with them; we must move quickly in the matter of your friend. Are you up for a cremation?'

'We Christians do not do cremations,' du Cleuxnz argued, 'For how does the body resurrect on the Last Day?'

'Doesn't it say in your holy book that you'd get a new one anyway, fashioned after your God?'

He thought, 'Well, yes.'

'Then, never mind; what do you expect if you wish a clean return home? Do you have a container of some kind and your Lord's coat of arms somewhere?'

'I think I can accommodate,' du Cleuxnz muttered frantically looking around his belongings. A couple of members of the company had arrived. They were Nedbard Marcus Corry, a descendant of a Roman Briton and the distant Hastings cousin, Aolfe Sans-Brys arrived. They were sent by Jazin to find out what the delay was.

'We wanted to see what was going on,' Corry announced.

'Help me sort some things out. I need to prepare this fellow for a burning,' du Cleuxnz commanded. *He was, by now, at his wit's end.*

'Anything to help, my lord,' Sans-Brys complied.

They found a container, filled with a party pack.

'Ah, we were saving them for...,' Corry moaned.

The dragon snapped, 'You did not come on this trip for a holiday, did you?'

Corry looked up and nearly fainted. Sans-Brys caught him and slapped him round 'til he came to.

'Thanks, friend,' he said to him.

'No worries. It seems we have a job to do,' Sans-Brys replied.

Corry knew he went on this Crusade for a glorious experience, but he still had his *need.*

The body was prepared and quick prayer was said by du Cleuxnz, recalling the time of the Conquest and Landing, the Battle of Hastings and some personal time spent with Lord Hastings. The body was then lightly covered with a thin liner Corry had kicking round his kit. All was ready.

Derwint warned, 'Everyone step back.' The three Crusaders obeyed, still in awe and fear of this monstrous, yet generous creature.

A huge breathe was drawn, then he lavishly released a flame to end all flames. The trio remained 'til the bitter end, watching the body of Lord Hastings become as dusty as the sand.

The company was further out into the distance, probably wondering what happened to the pair sent out to find du Cleuxnz. The trio had waited on their friend with respect, to be certain he would receive the good sending off he deserved.

A few minutes later, the embers had died out and du Cleuxnz gathered the leftover ashes, now intermingled with some Eastern sand and put the lot into the container, now used as an urn. He lovingly wrapped the Hastings coat of arms around it for identification.

He gave the urn to the dragon, 'You know where to take this?'

'Yes, I do. Totteringstate, England. I know the way,' Derwint assured.

'Good luck to you,' du Cleuxnz waved goodbye, as the dragon swooped past him.

du Cleuxnz, Corry and Sans-Brys headed off to rejoin their line. *It would be a very long way through the desert.*

CHAPTER V

The Bondigon, Derwint, flew away with the urn toward the British Isles. The clouds held their contents well and reasonable weather remained, *for now.* After a month or so of flying, he took shelter in a region of France when the rains came. He had heard the fellow, whose remains the Bondigon carried, was originally from the Sur-Le-Merde area and thought it would be fitting to place the urn. However, no one of the family lived there anymore... just the peasants left behind who carried on their farm work. Derwint had realised that the dying wishes to be buried at Totteringstate needed to be fulfilled.

After a meal consisting of several rats which scurried in the cave Derwint occupied, the dragon gathered his strength to fly to the adopted land of Lord Hastings. Suddenly, there were twinges of excitement relaying within his system, *or were they...? Nah,* Derwint said to himself, and carried on. *It would not be long to reach Totteringstate...*

Two youthful lads were walking along tall stalks of grass and crop material. The mother walked beside them, admiring the worker's zeal. It was Lady Elthia, wife of the Lord William Hastings, with the two children, Roger John and Aelebrett, patrolling the grounds of Totteringstate. A local sign designated this parcel of land as such and Derwint began his descent.

Aelebrett saw a shadow on the ground that was not his. There was a far span of wings that glided along the wavy crops.

'Mother, look,' he shouted.

Elthia looked up, astonished, to find the Bondigon nearly on top of her party.

'Children, come close; let's go inside. Shit, we've spent months on this harvest!' *She was far from amused.*

The threesome were overtaken by a loud booming voice from the heavens.

'Elthia,' the voice spoke, 'do not be afraid.'

She was devout, and fiercely believed in God; yet she was abashed at the personal forwardness of the command. She stopped in her tracks and realised it was not a devotional calling, but a dragon with a message... *to her. What would a dragon want with me?* She looked up with her hand at her mouth in fear. *Perhaps it was God after all.*

As a courtesy, possibly unwilling, she shouted back, 'Yes, I am Elthia.'

'I have something for you. Your husband, William, had fallen on a crusade. I carry his remains for you.'

'Why are you carrying his remains? Where is the body?'

'I had to burn it for logistics' sake. It would be rather messy by now if I hadn't.'

'Quite.' Elthia was concerned. She recalled that cremation was not fancied in the Christian burial process as there would be no body left to resurrect on the Last Day. *Ah well, the distance paid for reason.*

The dragon headed for an outbuilding... the earlier twinges were becoming stronger and he had to become human... *fast.* He came in for a landing and hid quickly to change form. He returned, naked, carrying the Hastings urn.

'For you, my lady,' Derwint said, giving it to Elthia, who was taken aback.

'Didn't I just see a...,' she stuttered.

'Yes, you saw a dragon and now you see me. Nothing to fear.'

Her composure was quick, 'I will have to give this to the parish. I will ensure he gets a decent burial.' She put the urn down on the ground.

'We could have buried him in the sand, out East, but he would not have it.'

Elthia grew cross, 'Can ye blame him? I would never want to die in some inhospitable rubbish piece of dead earth if you asked me.' Her manner then relaxed. 'I so thank you for honouring my late husband's wishes.'

'Not many were so lucky. I can only carry so many urns,' Derwint gave her a wink, 'Erm, could I trouble you for some apparel? I, um....,' he started to blush.

'I think a blush is rich coming from you. I believe I have something suitable. Just one moment.' Elthia rushed to the house to find a cover up for the strange man.

Roger and Aelebrett went up to the dragon-turned-human to make acquaintance.

The elder son, Aelebrett, remarked, 'We thought you would burn us out.' Then, he pointed to the urn, and asked, 'So, that's father, then?'

'I am sorry to come upon you so suddenly and frightful, and yes, your father's in there,'

Derwint replied as he saw Elthia returning with the needed garment.

'I think this should be useful. It belonged to my father,' she said.

'Why, thank you for your kindness, Elthia.' Derwint put on the Saxon tunic. It was slightly big, but it would do.

Aelebrett chimed in, 'Do you have a name?'

'Yes, oh, I do apologise. My name is Derwint.'

'That's a funny name for a dragon.'

'I am not an ordinary dragon. I am a Bondigon.'

It was Roger's turn for inquisitiveness, 'What's a Bondigon?'

Embarrassment shaded Derwint's face. Elthia saved the day, knowing of his *personal* issue.

'Aelebrett, take your brother to the house and wait for me there. I will be alright. Derwint means no harm.'

'Well, yes, Mother, for he did bring our father's ashes back.' Aelebrett agreed.

The sons walked off to the house. Aelebrett tried to explain the stranger's quirks to his brother. Then, they both started to laugh as they entered into the dwelling.

Derwint and Elthia were alone.

'So you understand what I am?'

'I think so,' Elthia said, 'I saw a flying *something* in the sky and then suddenly, I am clothing a man!'

'I'm a Bondigon. I go through a monthly cycle, like you do, but for a different reason. I need to mate with someone, and fast, ere I die,' he explained.

'Wow. I never would believe in a thrillion years I would be talking to a Bondigon, or dragon of any nature. I might be accused of witchery.'

'As I am presently human, you will be unharmed. You are speaking with your fellow man. It is rather sparse in this region, no?'

'The village itself is some distance away. About half a morning's ride, that way,' she pointed to another signpost stating the obvious.

'I see. Now, this is important. I do not wish to fulfil my desire with you, as I respect you, my lady. As I did you good service by bringing your husband home to you, please tell me where is the nearest tavern, public house… erm, brothel, even?'

'We do have a tavern in the village, Derwint, called *The Branched Flurry* along Wilset Green. They do have accommodations, I believe, and I am sure they could find someone for you to suffer your need.'

'That is most helpful, Lady Elthia, and I thank you, with all my heart.'

'No worries, it's just a monthly.'

'Yea, but you lose blood. I can lose my life.'

'Oh, since you put it that way...'

'Fare thee well, Elthia.' Derwint walked toward Totteringstate village. Elthia picked up the urn and brought it into the house, where the children were eagerly waiting for her return.
'What an odd fellow,' Roger quipped.

'Not really, once you get to know him,' Elthia defended, as she entered.

'I bet it was weird to chat up a real dragon,' Aelebrett remarked.

'It was, I confess, a most interesting exchange. Yet, we live in a time where the interesting is all around us. It depends upon how we interpret the interesting. I, for one, do not think it is wrong in any way,' she defended.

The family paused for few minutes. Elthia prophesied, 'Ready or not, there may be a spot of trouble with him,'.

Her prophesy was not unfounded. Late in the evening, news got around that there was a fiery incident in the village and a winged creature was seen flying off in haste.

At least she knew she would not be getting that tunic back in a hurry.

(Then the next morning, Elthia took her constitutional and nearly tripped on a familiar garment.)

Part II

Roger Alexander Woodes-Hastings

AD 1260s

Chapter VI

I attended worship at Totteringstate Parish Church on a visit to Totteringstate with my girlfriend, Elizabethia Mary Woodes. She was a peasant, yet she had not fallen (morally); she was lowly and remained lowly... (though her father had other plans, as an *upwardly mobile* peasant). She was an average native, with her roots firmly planted in England's soil. But, for all I knew, her family could have dwelled here longer, ages and ages past.

Her father, Alfith Cliveton Woodes, was a tradesman in straw mattresses. He sold them in the market in Totteringstate at Wilset Green, even though they were made in Dumfushire. They caught on well and soon, everybody wanted one. There were plenty of resources, and, astute as he was, began to use bird's feathers as stuffing. He was doing fine and kept his occupation intact and I believed he climbed a few notches up the status. However, most people kept him in his place and *made him remember it.*

We sat side by side, as we in Woolanshire were a progressive group, though traditionally devout. To celebrate Mass together in unity was central to the whole experience. I did not get distracted by Elizabethia's beauty... *it just added to the beauty of the holy worship.*

I closed my eyes for a bit, as I heard the prayerful litanies and smelt the warmth of the incense from nave to altar. By this time, I reopened them, and then went a-rovin' to view the many memorials to my aristocratic family, the Hastings, beginning with William. William came over from Sur-Le-Merde with his namesake, the Duke of Normandy, to conquer and settle the land... (*all the land*, so said our motto). His tomb was elaborate; the story handed down was that he died during an early Crusade and returned, by dragon, in an urn. Thus, no body was left for his tomb. This did not deter the family from putting up a special effigy of him anyway, along with his cherished wife, Elthia. *I was unsure about the dragon bit, though.*

William had assimilated well into the native culture and oversaw the pig farm he continued on from Sur-Le-Merde. There was a plaque inscribed which described him in Latin, *Meminisse a Genitore Suo* (translated as *A Progenitor to Remember)*. I was most proud to be descended from him.

There were more plaques commemorating the many offspring that flew under the Hastings' banner: Aelebrett and Roger John (from whom I am descended), plus various offspring who died young. Then came those noting my parents, Roger William and Mathilda, who died over the past ten years. I still had my twin brother, who was a senior Cluniac monk, called Wilfin Aeldric Hastings. He entered the local monastery from a young age and had lived there ever since. Yet it did not stop visitations from myself to bring him up to speed on recent events or news which concerned him. And he returned such favours to me, in turn, when possible.

My late father, Roger William, had ruined our family name and status, by having an affair with a peasant woman called Anna Elderfynne. She was the only surviving daughter of John Elderfynne, who originally was called John Elder Fynne. He left his home in Ireland, lived in Scotland for a few years and finally ended up in England where, due to a clerical error in a record book, he was known as John Elderfynne. He accepted this and moved on with the new name. The rest is unknown; as far as I can tell, it could probably be dodgy, or maybe was a spell of restlessness on his part.

Roger William had been pretty faithful to Mathilda over the years, but for a bad spell he was going through. The pig farm was doing fairly, but things could have been better. The home at Totteringstate weathered a little, but remained steady. Yet, he was a drinker and enjoyed it so. With the drink, he got a little uneasy with himself and things got a bit messy. *Miss Elderfynne was in the tavern at that time and he went up to her...*

The end result was our family being removed from our home to live in Dumfushire. We were allowed to keep the farm (and *work* on it), as well as the Hastings name, but without privilege. Miss Elderfynne was sent away and had a son. They never returned, and there was no news of them since. This was the beginning of the new lineage that descended off our line of the family.

I further reflected and recalled when we had to leave Totteringstate Hall to a distant cousin, Sir Pym Aolfe (still pronounced 'Alf') Sans-Brys, who looked after the estate in my stead. I was greatly fond of Totteringstate, having grown up there and I was determined to reclaim my lost heritage. I thought about it in made-up verse:

A wild hair up the Hastings tree
Was plucked forth to fall upon me.
And I wanted to make the Hastings name great again;
It will come, ye shall see!

Once my parents and myself were expelled from our home, we ended up living on the pig farm in Dumfushire. *We were aristocrats living as peasants*, domiciled at Hastings Court. This dwelling was built by The Progenitor, William, which continued to house many of the on-site staff. Cousin Sans-Brys thought it was for the best and allowed us to remain on as workers. As the dominant males of our family, it was a rotten humiliation to my father and myself. But, we tried our best. Personally, I firmly believed this was the beginning of his end which led to an early grave. I, on the other hand, made many friends among the workers and enjoyed a sense of family. *Thankfully, I was able to adapt quickly to the new circumstance.*

I carried on ransacking my mind as more prayers were being said and I was getting restless. Elizabethia tugged at my tunic sleeve, 'My lord, the service has concluded. Shall we go forth? It's a lovely day and Buckingham and the rest will be waiting outside for us.'

I found it truly amusing that she would consider me her *lord*, as if our peasant status had not affected us, and we were yet unwed. *I guessed she said it out of affection for me.*

'We shall, my love,' I cooed back to her. I wanted to give her a kiss, but that type of 'peace be with you' was not allowed in such a place. I rose to put on my cloak; my love waited for me on the side of the pew, smiling and chatting to the local villagers.

Suddenly, a call heralded us from our current exchange. It was Cateliffe.

'Oh come now, Rog,' he pleaded, 'Make a short shrift of it; we long to be ahead of you at the supper table.'

Another fellow worker and close friend, Buckingham, moaned, 'Rog, you coming?' He went 'round to find us and caught a glimpse.

I raised my head to face him, 'Yes, Bucks, I'll be there.'

Now, it was Nay-Smith's turn, 'You look like you've got your hands full and by the Holy Rood, I'll be first at the supper table.' He glanced at Cateliffe, who could not help but smile.

When we left the building, we snuck off to one side and I gave her a real-time grand kiss. She loved it; I loved it; God didn't care... *and no one else did either*, for they all knew about my love for Elizabethia.

'That's love for you, but on the Lord's Day?' Cateliffe sounded astonished.

'Eh, why not? They do go on about loving thy neighbour,' Wilset quipped.

Dormer Wilset was new to our group. He was born on Wilset Green, Totteringstate, when his family went to the market there. There were other friends and co-workers I associated with, who were meeting with us back on the farm in Dumfushire. There was Raif Buckingham, Lovelby Cateliffe, Stanley Nay-Smith, Drew Brackbury, Laurence Tarquinne, Bakerleigh Tudmond, and Pam-Anne Portaclaire. As I had no family of my own, other than Wilfin, my friends made up for the purpose. I enjoyed working with them and having them as social company. They knew my cousin was very fair toward me when he put my parents and I into the pig farming trade as workers. *Someday, I planned to change all that,* and I will become the lord as intended, with my friends beside me.

We hurried back to Hastings Court for our Sunday meal.

The next day we met at our local tavern, *The Incensed Rose*, after a long day at the farm. I found it difficult to withhold my desire for eating among my friends, who, like our charges, were ravenous pigs themselves. We gathered at our usual table upstairs (as there were many of our party), with Elizabethia and Pam-Anne. Buckingham and I went to order our drinks and meals. Thankfully, our toils on the farm allowed us to 'live a little', despite our lesser status. *Well, we spent much of our time in mud and filth; at least it paid our bills.*

Whilst waiting for the drinks, Buckingham spoke to me, 'Big market day ahead; we've got lots of meat to sell and rents to pay.'

'Yea, I think they're due now.'

'It is a good set-up; everyone pitches in.'

'There's much to be said for it,' I concurred, 'Yet, we live simply and do not waste our time with nonsense. Good work and prayer, that's all we need.'

'Umm,' Buckingham nodded.

Our drinks arrived and we had assistance from the staff to bring them to our table. The food would come later.

I helped pass out the ales and put away my coins. This round was on me, as a thank you for the hard work everyone put in. It turned out that my fellow workers were experimenters as well, as Nay-Smith revealed.

'I was thinking about various uses for pig fat and sell it on. I know it is not the nicest of substances, but Cateliffe and I had explored possibilities.'

My eagerness got the better of me, 'And what did ye find, then?'

Cateliffe interjected, 'It can be used for cooking.'

'Insulation,' Tudmond offered.

'That's right,' I congratulated, 'Mixed with straw, it could work.'

Brackbury thought of an idea, 'What about as a cleaning product?'

Buckingham scoffed, 'Bracks, no one bathes often 'round here.'

'Maybe we should start,' Brackbury continued, 'We could solidify the fat into bars and put scents within it such as lavender, rosewater, or whatever one fancies.'

'What would you call it and where does one get these spices from,' Tarquinne argued, 'We're not the types to go out and buy that sort of thing.'

Brackbury schemed, 'But we do know where we could buy it, or get someone else to, at least. If we have this product, we might do well for ourselves. Might be appealing for the ladies, too!' He gazed at Pam-Anne and Elizabethia.

'I would buy it,' Pam-Anne spoke up, 'I do not want to smell like pig shit all day.'

Elizabethia nodded, 'I would too... so I can have my Roger.' She smiled at me and gave me a kiss.

'All right, all right,' Wilset broke out, 'You two can take that elsewhere.' He turned to see a couple of fellows bringing out the meals. 'Our food is here, anyway.'

We all began our meal with a quick prayer, then dug in.

'So what would you call these pieces of acceptably smelling bathing fat?' Nay-Smith piped up after a sip of ale.

'Fullonum?' Buckingham contributed.

I mulled over the idea over my wine. We carried on eating silently, respecting each other's manners.

'Fullonum it is,' I conceded, realising a connection, 'It is actually Latin for soap, or at the very least, a cleansing product.'

Tudmond was enjoying his meal very much, 'This here is good meat.'

'Course it is good meat; it is our meat!' I could not believe Tudmond's forgetfulness. I figured that it comes from being a *real* peasant.

'You sell meat here too, Rog?' Buckingham, though unrelated, had a touch of Tudmond's attribute.

'Yea, Bucks, I do,' I stated, ''Tis a guaranteed income. I have a deal with this tavern which dates back to the Conquest.' Dear William was very shrewd and knew how to make a coin or two. *At least being his descendant was beneficial to me.* Despite my family having to become part of the peasantry, the arrangement William made long ago had remained. No reason for prejudice when there is money to be made and people to feed for many a celebration or a plain slap-up meal.

'Ah, that's it, good thinking,' Elizabethia smiled and winked at me.

I took notice of it and asked her if she could help me at the market stall.

'I could,' she assured, kissing me, 'And I hope it continues our path toward marriage.'

'I hope it does, as you are my intended, but we must work toward it. We will need to save up.' I returned her kiss.

The group looked disapproving for a bit, but understood the nature of our love. Pam-Anne was slightly jealous, so she reached for the nearest fellow (who happened to be Tudmond) and gave him a kiss which lasted as long as mine and Elizabethia's.

Wilset was unnerved and moaned, 'Oh, please!'

'Pipe down,' Buckingham scolded him, 'Let them love, for who will love ye?'

Cateliffe sniggered to himself. Wilset glared at him and everyone howled.

Brackbury got philosophical, 'A miss like that can be forgiven, if one had a miss like that sitting beside you.'

I blushed and felt strongly about my love.

'Still, it's not for the table in front of, well, you know,' Wilset attempted to argue.

'Why, Wilset, have ye no one to love?' Buckingham teased.

Wilset then glared daggers at Buckingham. The table resumed its normal sense of chatter and relaxation as we whiled a few hours there before returning to the farm.

CHAPTER VII

Wednesday was our Market Day for the village of Totteringstate, where its normally sleepy atmosphere sprang to life. My family had earned a good reputation here, from the pig farm, and dispensation of its produce to the locals. Though *The Incensed Rose* allocated a good part of the income we earned, the rest depended on Market Day.

We set up at Wilset Green, among many other stall holders that came from other areas around Woolanshire and Dumfushire. There was healthy competition betwixt us all and thankfully, *it was friendly*; anything fierce was reserved for the larger, ruthless cities.

The market was filled with stalls which crammed every inch of Wilset Green. There were many items in the stalls, such as food and drink, textiles, weaponry and metals, animal hides of various types, candlesticks, amongst others. Our local sheriff, Richard DeMoro, oversaw the weekly event to prevent any abusive entanglements. Many people came to the market from Dumfushire and Woolanshire, as it was aimed toward local interests, and everyone was dependent on everyone else to keep the system going. It could get hectic with crowds and, at times, I found it most overwhelming.

Nay-Smith, Buckingham and Cateliffe put out our products, freshly killed and Tudmond handled the lard buckets. I stood by, whilst my colleagues did much of the work. I preferred to pack the items and collect the money from customers. It was nice to see the potential for new customers, as well as the same lot who keep refreshing their weekly orders.

However, this Market Day was one I would rather forget. An elder lady, who I'd never seen before, was walking along the aisles with a young girl. The lady looked fairly well-to-do in her curtain-material dress and exquisite head covering. I thought the child could be related, but I did not enquire. The lady's voice, though, had the ring of one of the more aggressive female fishmongers.

The elder shouted to the girl, 'Stop slouching! How many times had I told you to present yourself?!'

'I'm trying not to, Nan, but your shopping is quite a challenge to carry,' the girl protested.

The girl kept walking. She had an odd look about her, with a page boy haircut, baggy tunic (which hid her early bloom and gave her no figure whatsoever), dark hose and a darker cloak to match. *'Tis a pity for such prospective beauty to be lying so dormant... there was nothing complimentary about her.*

The elder lady was persistent. 'Good God, Maisel, you need to put more back into it!'

'Please, Nan, I am trying. Just let me get on with it!' *It was obvious the girl was struggling badly.*

'Well, you do not look it,' the old lady changed the subject, still chastising, 'You are nearly sixteen and you have not found a husband yet!'

'Stop bugging me about that, please.'

'Well, in my day, I had a match before I could walk,' she boasted.

'It is not like that now, and I will know when it happens, alright?'

'If you wore your hair more effeminately, you could attract someone. Who would want a girl like you, looking a right mess?'

Maisel turned around, 'Nan, it is YOU who wanted my hair cut in this boyish fashion, and making me wear tunics twice my size so that they do not fit properly.'

'It is practical and you play with your hair too much,' Nan retorted back.

'NAN!' Maisel shouted which a force that stilled the market chatter.

'Maisel, hold your tongue!'

She stuck out her tongue and clasped the tip with her fingers.

'Cheeky. If you were more attentive and attractive, you would not be in the mess you are in.'

'What, living with you? That is an ageing gospel!'

Nan wanted to strike out at the girl, but in public, she had to keep decorum. Sheriff DeMoro already had his keen eye on the woman and was not amused at her nefarious attitude toward her charge.

Maisel was deep-down furious with her nan's terrier-like snapping. A few moments had passed... she had an idea and waited for 'Nan' to kick off again.

... and kick off she did.

'Another thing I do not like is that you have a fresh mouth,' she said, as predicted, 'You never smile, so it is a wonder nobody likes you. You are most selfish and not a nice person at all.'

Maisel did not react and let Nan rant as much as she pleased, mostly complaining about the faults the child possessed. She did not think her elder meant it on purpose, as such, but the public humiliation had been difficult to cope with over the years of it being done to her.

The young girl had had enough of Nan's whinging about her and cried out in a loud voice, pointing with accusation, 'WITCH!'

I could scarcely believe my ears; my co-workers looked at me and at one another, dumbfounded.

Sheriff DeMoro had also had enough of this squelching nonsense doled out by this elder lady. Although she looked the big part in society, *she was no better than anyone else* and he figured she was calling attention to herself. He felt he got more than he bargained for when he volunteered for this market run, distracting him from more important duties elsewhere. He moaned and sighed inside, taking courage and strength from God. He exhaled one last breath before he pulled himself up inside and got on with the job.

A deputy called Nellington came up to Nan to restrain her. DeMoro grimly went up to Maisel, 'It had been many a year before someone was accused of witchery in these parts. Have you evidence of the same?'

'Isn't the arguments and critical abuse enough? You must have heard us, as we are not lightweight in volume,' Maisel argued.

'Well, 'tis only an argument. Most family members always get into tiffs of this sort. I see no reason to...'

Maisel cut the Sheriff off, 'No! This has been going on for years... since the year Dot! We have always been arguing.'

'What is your name, miss?'

'Maisel Larke, sir.'

'Do you have a place to go, Miss Larke, whilst we investigate the matter?'

'Ummm, no, I do not. I've been living with my grandparents since the year Dot.'

'The year Dot obviously had not been a good year for you, then,' the Sheriff conceded.

'No, sir,' she said meekly.

I entered the foray, with Nay-Smith behind me.

'I can help, Sheriff,' Nay-Smith offered.

The Sheriff seemed dubious and questioned him. 'Can you? Do you know this girl?'

'Not personally, but I have seen and heard the goings on between the girl and the elder woman.'

'And to your knowledge, the relationship was most unsatisfactory?'

'Not a kind word was spoken between them, sir,' Nay-Smith confirmed.

'I can vouch for this too, your Honour,' I piped up, 'I believe she would be of great service to us.'

DeMoro asked me, 'Who are you?'

'I am Roger Hastings and this is Stanley Nay-Smith of Dumfushire.'

'You two from that pig farm, correct?'

'Aye,' I assured.

'Alright. I know you lot have a good solid reputation in this area, and I am certain she will be safe with you. Go on, take her,' Sheriff DeMoro handed the girl over to us, 'But, if I need her during my investigation, I may need to call her in.'

'Fine,' I said, then I turned to Maisel, 'Is this good for you? Would you like to help on our stall?'

'Yes,' she affirmed, 'At least it would be a respite from *her*.'

'Then I leave her in good hands. Deputy Nellington will see to the grandmother and I will be in touch. Thank you for your cooperation.' Sheriff DeMoro shook my hand and walked away.

Nay-Smith spoke to Maisel. 'Was it always like that with her? Did she always deride you?'

'Yes she did,' Maisel was downcast, 'I only called her a witch cos I was tired of her antics with me.'

'Sounded quite fierce.'

'It was...,' her voice trailed off into sadness.

I had to do something to break this foul mood. We had work to do. I suggested, 'Ummm, are you up for selling some meat?'

'Great, I would love that!' She gave me a hug.

'Whoa, girl, I'm taken,' I warned.

'Oh, you're married? I do apologise.'

'Not yet, but I have been courting a young lady for some time. We do plan to get married. We have good staff where we are and you should fit in nicely.'

Nay-Smith stepped in to distract her away from me... *he knew*. 'Let me take you to our stall, Mais...'

'Maisel,' she said.

'Maisel. Nice name,' Nay-Smith carried on, leading her to the stall.

The tone of the market had quieted down as we worked hard to sell our meat. I went off to search for Elizabethia, who took a break from the stall, when I noticed her with a young child approaching her person. The child spent some time around her, for some odd reason and I watched for the next move. She shooed the child away from her. Elizabethia did not have anything elaborate as such, but I knew she kept a money bag secured well on her belt, and hidden inside an inner pocket within the folds of her complex dress. The belt itself was visible and seemed to be the target of the young child, who apparently was trying to lift it from her. *Apparently, he was trained that a belt could hold up more than just clothing.*

'Thia, your side,' I called out to her.

She jolted and turned round to find that young kid running away to its mother, thankfully, with nothing. She instinctively put her hand on her side and *phew*, her property was still present. The kid attempted his scheme upon her anyway, secure or not, goaded by the mother, but this time with no success. The mother soon afterwards, got very cross with the child and with herself, knowing *she did not get the goods*, so to speak.

Another shouting match ensued, this time between Elizabethia and this mother. It was a similar ranting, such as the fuss the grandmother made over poor Maisel. Yet, in due credit and fortitude on Elizabethia's part, it was a one-way rant; my dearest love did not even rise to the bait of this horribly sounding tirade.

'You are a very rude person, telling my child to shoo; You should not be around young children nor care for them; you should be ashamed of yourself,' the mother raved against my beloved.

The argument went on and on; *in my humble opinion, here was a time to cry 'Witch'!* Elizabethia tuned the screaming raver out of her mind. She faced me, holding me quite tightly and kept calling my name, like a litany. This lady did not look nor sound English. Her overall attitude and composure was not English. I reckoned her to be a foreigner, as one does not do such a thing here. Our Market Days are usually quiet, but for the noise of sellers and happy customers (for the most part).

The child remained standing by his mother's bag, empty handed when the mother tried to flee the scene, once the nonsense had passed. Too many people gathered by now and the quick-witted DeMoro was on the scene, *again.*

'When it rains, it pours,' he said to me, 'What's the trouble now?'

I pointed to the child and mother and several witnesses came up to secure Elizabethia's innocence.

'Another one to pasture,' DeMoro sighed, 'Let's go.'

The mother protested, in vain, 'No, I'm innocent, that lady there was bothering my child.'

A witness raged, 'The child started it and the mother allowed her child to wander toward strangers.'

'He's only a child,' the mother wailed.

Another witness complained, 'Yea, and where were ye then? Why weren't you looking after him? Why wasn't he restrained upon yer person, eh?'

The desperate mother realised she had lost and tried, again, to run for it. The crowd prevented her and she ended up in the Sheriff's custody.

He shrugged and walked away with both child and parent. *Another investigation*, he thought, *it never ends being a Sheriff.*

'What a day,' he confessed to me, 'I'll be glad to see the back of it.'

'Godspeed and good luck to ye,' I waved, 'Have a cup of ale, on me.' I gave him a few shillings for his trouble.

'I'll need it, thanks,' came his reply.

The crowd dispersed from that conundrum and I went back to my stall, holding Elizabethia tightly, and kissed her in reassurance of my continuing love for her.

'How goes it?' I enquired of my co-workers.

'Quite good, Rog,' Buckingham admitted, 'Despite the disruptive events.' The table had less carcasses upon it, proving the day was not in vain. Cateliffe was busy wiping down the tables to keep them reasonably tidy. *Handling carcasses was a messy business.*

'Very well,' I complimented, then turning to Tudmond, 'And you?'

Tudmond tipped over the barrel to reveal only dregs and scraps of fat left over at the bottom.

'You've been busy,' I smirked, as he gave me the takings to pool together with Buckingham's. I usually dole it out amongst my co-workers, but we do it in the comfort of Hastings Court... *one would not like to flash one's cash about.*

CHAPTER VIII

Sir Pym Aolfe Sans-Brys stood within the walls of Totteringstate Hall, evermore relishing his victory. From a maternal offshoot of the de Hastings line, this cousin felt compelled to enjoy the spoils of a bad decision. Roger William Hastings was disgraced by infidelity with the lower order and he and his family had to leave their home at Totteringstate. Now, Pym was Lord of Totteringstate, at least by default, *but through no fault of his own.*

He was in his mid-forties, yet unwed; a tall man, but thin from being over fussy with his food; sand coloured short hair, blue eyes and chiselled features which brought an energetic stir to the ladies. He was a knight and a soldier in a recent Crusade. He loved a good fight. His ancestor, Aolfe, came to England with the Norman invasion, along with his cousin, William de Hastings (the 'de' bit was dropped from the name later on). They went on an early Crusade together, during which William had died en-route to the East. Aolfe had endured it to the end and took a few good men with him. He treasured fulfilment and flew his way into the various towns that the Crusaders had entered, and did his bit for Christendom.

However, upon reflection, Pym later recalled *Aolfe never returned from that Crusade* and thanked Heaven that he left several children behind, one from whom he was descended.

Pym also thought about his unwed status and wanted thoroughly to do something about it. He had a roving eye amongst the pretty ladies of Woolanshire County, but firmly rejected those from Dumfushire. Yet, there was one girl he had a sight for... Elizabethia Woodes... the girl who was intended for me, Roger Alexander Hastings (Roger William's son).

As a lord of Totteringstate, Pym was in a cosy position. He enjoyed taking rides out to Dumfushire, to gloat at me, *the real heir of Totteringstate Hall.*

He liked the primal nature of the people there and the work they did, by the sweat of their brow. He soon caught sight of my girlfriend, Elizabethia; she was taking a walk in the garden, after her daily chores 'round the farm.

He approached her with caution and stealth, scheming an endless scheme of hope to have this girl for himself. Pym did not care a whit for anyone, *especially me...* yet she might admonish Pym. Pym scoffed the thought and boldly forwarded himself on his horse toward her.

He approached her, dismounting, and asked in his genteel manner, 'How ye do, miss?'

'Fine, thank you. Phew, what a day.' Elizabethia sat down on the Holy Rock of Dumfushire. It was believed by locals that it held special powers to assist them in their windswept, tumultuous days. Some thought it could bring them good fortune. Another group thought God Himself had touched it and saw it as a sign... others, however, thought *that* group saw the sign from a nearby tavern and the myth went from there.

'You've been busy,' Pym noted, looking at her scruffy hands.

'Aye, 'tis so. What's a fine fellow like you doing in our district? You are in charge of Totteringstate, are you not?' Her eyes held suspicion.

'Just happen to be passing through, my lady,' he cooed mockingly, *with a purpose.*

'Can't imagine why *you* would want to pass through here.'

'Why? Why, then? And why not! So I may see the most beautiful lass of Dumfushire.'

'You've got a nerve,' Elizabethia flared up, 'I am promised to Roger and besides, I am not of your station.'

'Indeed you are not, as yours is merely up the road, and mine is in the next county over,' Pym snidely remarked.

'Surely, ye jest, sir,' she said coarsely.

'On the contrary. Never before have I been serious in all my life.'

'And what life is that, I wonder? To take over your cousin's estate?'

'Ho-ho, my dear, 'tis nay like that. The father was at fault and I was called into look after the property. Maybe I will buy it and think upon a nice girl to settle in with. Could ye be that girl, lass?'

Elizabethia felt abashed and shocked at Pym's progressiveness upon her. 'It grieves me to think you haven't a girl of your own.'

'Well, I think low, so as to look better than the girl.'

'A right peacock ye are!' She spat on the ground.

'Yea and a right reverend too, but you don't see me spitting on the floor about it! Do you know I have the gall to put you over my lap and spank ye.'

'Oh yea, and my Roger will come for you with a vengeance... and may he kicketh thy butt!'

'Roger, Roger! Why have him, when you've got... you know... *me*,' he slyly winked at her. He then sniggered and awaited her response.

'Why, I ought to,' Elizabethia attempted to slap him, but he grabbed her wrist before impact.

'Now, now, my young girl... or are you really old in disguise?' He continued his playful stance, annoying and torturous as it was, 'What does Roger got that I don't?'

'He's untainted, unblemished, and pure in every way. He is a good man, despite what his father had done. One doesn't tar another with the same brush. I love him; he loves me,' she defended.

'Oh yea, who told y'that?'

'He did, and I believe,' she snapped.

'Oh,' he went on to further mock her, 'And I believe in Father, Son and Holy Ghost, and on the Last Day, Man is to be saved.'

Elizabethia was aghast, and screamed, 'Infidel!'

'Yea, I'm an infidel, as you call me, and my ancestor fought against them in the East, as did I,' Pym explained and gave her a raspberry.

''Tis a wonder you survived, then, sir.'

''Tis a wonder you've got Roger. You can have me.'

'Why the hell would I want you?'

'Because, deep down, you want to better yourself,' he explained, 'Deep down, you love me... for my excitement, my ecstasy, I can offer you the world, so much more than your pig farmer lover can. I will not set thee free. I want you to enter my Romeo'd brain and mash thyself therein.'

'What do y--,' Elizabethia was suddenly silenced as Pym grabbed her close and kissed her, roughly and rigorously, tongue and all.

'Ye bastard,' she cried, freeing herself from him, and wiping her mouth.

'Nay, I am no bastard, but I'd like one with--,' he got interrupted by a harsh slap in the face.

He looked at her with angry eyes, making his inner passion soar to the moon and back, *and possibly with a side trip to Totteringstate, girl in arms.*

'Ye bitch, I'll get thee and make thee mine,' he tore part of her dress and fumbled at the exposed naked flesh.

'Alas, I cannot make ye a fair proposal, but I'll not see me raped!'

'Rape ye, I will, for even us bastards get aroused.'

'No, please.' She knew it would be a horrid curse upon her to be defiled like this.

He pressed on, grabbing her into his arms once more to kiss her again. After a time, he had let go.

'You will not hear the end of this, sir,' Elizabethia warned.

Pym took it in stride, but did not care. He was intrigued and continued to scheme to see himself ingratiated with her, at all costs.

Meanwhile, Elizabethia left Pym to seek me at the farm, where I was helping Nay-Smith scrape up pig muck from a sty.

'Roger, Roger,' she exhaled a fervent breath from running, 'I've found you, at last!'

'My love, Elizabethia, how now? You seem harass'd.' I looked more closely and cried with bother, 'Christ, your dress!'

'Your cousin, Sans-Brys, attempted his own 'pon my person. I tried to hold the line, but he would not answer me appropriately.'

'But you are *my* woman!'

''Tis not a matter for thee to choose. He is above thee and will decide for himself.'

'Yea, but not by much,' I stated, 'Remember, *we* are the true inheritors of Totteringstate.'

'I know it, love,' she sighed, 'Pym would make such a sham of your belov'd estate. He even threatened to buy it! What are we to do?' Elizabethia sounded exasperated when Cateliffe, Nay-Smith and Buckingham turned up.

'Any problem here? Ye sound distress'd, ma'am,' Cateliffe said with concern in his voice and with respect to her.

'Nay, Cateliffe,' I assured, ''Tis but a family matter. Do pay it no heed.'

'Affairs of the family mean affairs of the heart,' Buckingham interjected, attempting to be clever.

I counterbalanced his meagre frivolity and asked, 'Where doth love enter 'pon this thorny path?'

Buckingham stared at me blankly, 'I haven't a clue, Rog.'

Nay-Smith came up with a plan and suggested, 'Why don't ye challenge the git? That wanker tore your lady's dress! 'Tis preposterous!'

'Let us see him work and enjoy the holy smell of indulgence thereof,' Cateliffe offered and cackled wildly with mirth, showing a gap-toothed smile.

'I'd like to see him proposing to anyone, knee-deep in shit,' Buckingham outwardly imagined and smiled.

I thought about it and felt Pym must be challenged. *Problem was, he was a challenge at the best of times.*

'A public engagement,' Cateliffe quickly stepped in.

I concluded, 'He is a warrior of sorts and I am quite handy with weapons and horses. Before my father fell from favour, he taught me a thing or two about fighting. Remember, my ancestor William came over with the Norman forces.'

'Yea, y'keep reminding us and all he got was a descendant living in pig shit,' Buckingham mocked.

Aye, he got me there, that Buckingham. Still, it was a menace to live like this when I knew *I could do better.* I must win back Totteringstate and marry Elizabethia. Perhaps something new could come of this.

CHAPTER IX

Some months had passed and autumn was due to arrive. I was thinking of a holiday, but not one of leisure. I wanted a spiritual quest, but did not want to venture far from home. *There was already a Crusader in our family, and it did not get him anywhere!* I thought about my twin brother, Wilfin, and decided to go on a retreat at the local monastery.

Usually, it wasn't the done thing to go off and make enquiries to the monks, who would normally ignore any undue outside influence. Yet, this was my brother and I wrote him a message anyway. I sent Nay-Smith on horse to deliver it.

Later, I got an affirmative response from Wilf, who had not seen me since our younger days. After many years isolated among fellow monks, he had the ability to (at last) break away and spend time with me... for he was about to enter a new phase in his religious life. Wilf was accepted to serve at Totteringstate Parish Church as a priest. I felt happy for him and hoped, perhaps, he could get myself and Elizabethia married.

The Cluniac monastery of St. Gillacott had been established since the Conquest, with a few monks in the Order accompanying the army of William, Duke of Normandy. William, my ancestor, had it built when he was granted the lands of Woolanshire and Dumfushire.

It became the monks' home since. It was situated on Woolanshire's border and a toll bridge was built on the monastery's grounds, over the river Syd, to cross into Dumfushire and back. It was manned and a monk would have the pleasure of collecting monies from those wishing to go betwixt the counties. The monies collected therefrom were used toward the monastery for repair work, food, linens and wool for clothing/bedding, parchment and quills and any extra would go directly to local charities. There was another toll bridge located at the village of Totteringstate as an alternative route. Monies collected from there served the community.

In the early days, there were about six monks to start, but as they set a hold on the community, the many who lived there had sent the children to the monastery for religious structure and a forever rigid life. They felt their younger children would get a better start there and these children developed well therein. Its numbers would later grow to about a hundred and continued to flourish.

Wilf loved the life there and found it of great comfort. Our family debacle did not affect him one bit, as he was ensconced within St. Gillacott's walls before it happened. The Cluniacs did not get much news from outside; most of the time it did not concern them. Their focus was on God and worship and they followed this with strict devotion. Of course, they rested and had meals together. Wilf loved his weekly gardening duties and occasional stint at the toll bridge. The fresh air had done him some good and cleared his mind to continue his silent prayers beyond the mainstream Masses that were said over the various periods of the day.

The strict regime, though, was not for everybody and most outsiders found it relieving to think that *the monks did it, so one did not have to.* Comfort was not easy to come by at the best of times and for the Cluniac monks, the lack thereof became *the* way of life. So clean, so clinical, and so spartan! I knew, in my human weakness, I could still want the good things in life, despite my status being knocked down a peg. I also liked a good woman. *There, that would disqualify me immediately!* Wilf had known about Elizabethia from my letters to him, but never mentioned her in return. He took his vows seriously and was on another plane of life; I was too boorish in my thinking and messed about with my mates and Elizabethia for much of my time (when not working).

I met up with Wilf at the toll bridge. As a monk, he was not required to pay the fee, but, of course, I was and I did. *It was for a good cause, anyway.*

My shaggy haired twin stood there in his simple finery, all in black, but for a cord around his waist with a hooded black cloak and a rosary in his hand. If he were not my twin, I would be quite scared of such a figure; *he looked intimidating in all that black!* Only the sandy shade of hair atop his head contrasted, along with his pale, pasty-coloured skin. He looked exactly like me, but an opposite, more humbler and poorer (*but I doubted, with all that prayer, that he was poor*). His lifestyle was for the pure in heart and this did not come easy for us folk 'round here.

I came up to him, with a quick step, and we embraced.

'Brother Wilfin,' I cried, not realising the punning intention.

'Brother Roger,' he returned the favour, pun-free.

We looked at one another. I saw myself no better than he, in the unsavoury fabrics clothed about my person.

He took pity, 'You are poor, indeed, brother. Is the farm on the wilt?'

'Never better, actually,' I explained, 'I've adapted well since Father's decline and kept things in hand. These clothes were all I could find that did not linger among pig shit. You are aware of his decline?'

'It had been too long, Roger. It is a pitiful shame this happened. Lucky I was taken in well beforehand. How's Dumfushire treating you? It must be a long way from Totteringstate Hall. Who took over the estate?'

'Our cousin, Sans-Brys. He lives were we once did and manages the estate, yet I have been living in simplistic splendour. I will not give in to extreme poverty. If people want us to live as low-lives, then fine... but I will work to get us to live well and back to Totteringstate.'

'Your faith does you credit, but if God wanted us to live in poverty and simplicity, then that is His will,' Wilf commented.

'No, Wilf, that was *Father's* will and *his* mistake,' I argued.

Wilf felt abashed, then composed himself. 'Still, you have come to join us for retreat?'

'Yes, but I did not bring much,' I had a small bag with extra changes of undergarments.

'We can supply some linen and a robe for you. You brought enough. Come, let us walk and get you settled in. You can share my bed.'

I wondered, 'Do you sleep alone, normally?'

'Sometimes, but when we have a guest, the sleeping arrangements get altered to fit accordingly.'

'How much longer will you stay before your time at the Totteringstate Parish begins?'

'Another month. The Head is allowing me this one-time-only visit with you before I depart. I would like to see you more often.'

'I do too, and wish you much luck in your endeavour. I really want you to officiate at my wedding.'

'I'd be delighted to, Roger. By the way, how is your little princess?'

I grinned at his complimentary sarcasm. 'Fine, but remember she is of lesser class, not a princess.'

'Fine. An *upwardly mobile* peasant... what does her father do, again?'

'Mattress maker and seller,' I answered.

'Ah, a merchant type, then. Very upward and mobile. I wonder... ummm, we could do with some new filling for our beds,' he thought aloud.

'My dear Wilfin, you are as worldly as you are saintly.'

'Well we can't always be perfect. If we were, we would cast God out of a job, wouldn't we?'

Ha-ha, very funny, Wilf!

We walked past the ornate gate and entered the Norman built Cluniac monastery. I was taken through the main sanctuary, toward the dormitories where Wilf had sorted some appropriate clothing for me to wear for my visit. This consisted of under-linen, and a plain black robe with a rope tie round the waist. I also had a dark cloak to wear outside. *At least my shoes were sufficient*, I sighed. I did not mind dressing and living as a monk for a few days; it would be more difficult to trade one's regular lifestyle to this, as I found out quickly during the course of the stay.

CHAPTER X

I spent my visit following the monk's routines, which consisted of bell ringing, chanted prayer, sparse mealtimes (by my standard), more chanted prayer, more Mass, more prayer (solitary, this time), occasional work such as gardening or scribing books (but this was once a week, usually), and then more prayer before finally turning in for bed.

Their bedtimes were quite early at the nineteenth hour of the day (which is seven o'clock at night to me and usually the time I spent with my friends or Elizabethia). They awoke at the third hour past midnight and that really tried me. On the farm, our wake-up time was usually five or six (or sometimes seven, if we really wanted to push it!) For my dear brother, Wilf, I was willing to go along with it for the time being.

I arrived in time for evening prayer and meal that followed. Bedtime was shortly thereafter so, I did not get to spend much time with Wilf, like I wanted. I respected this and hoped sometime, I will get to spend a wee bit of time with him. We needed a good catching up.

The praying was most comforting, with a one line verse lasting for some time. The chanting alone did not need musical accompaniment, as the monk's voices remained in tune. The duration of the service, I found a little awkward; *but I knew this was only for a short spell for me.* My mind meandered within this pool of prayer...

There was so much soul searching, praying and silent contemplation to be had in a dim light of the main church, whose small coloured window had the only light shining through....to ask one's Maker for mercy and absolution; abstinence of endless sin? Living itself is sin, or could be if unchecked. There had always been a God, for anything else is prepost'rous! One's soul drowned a pool of thought, of freedom of thought no one else could ever see or feel.

A different language rang out within this holy sanctuary, not in conversation... but in prayer. The ancient prayers in Latin were most enhancing. No other language said it more than, *Gloria In Excelsis Deo* -- ah, so breath-taking! One received strength from the Cross and personally one could not get any better than this.

My thoughts remained as pure as humanly possible, as I negotiated my way through the Latin plain-chants. I joined in, as Wilf encouraged me to do, and set my mind on the straight and narrow. A passing desire for Elizabethia trespassed during the service, but as long as I kept this to myself, I did not think Heaven would glance at it. I truly missed her and could not wait to bask in her presence.

My eyes roved within the dark sanctuary, with a fading sun giving its final say into the latticed and stained glass windows. Some of the stained glass depicted biblical scenes in living colour. The incense filled the room with sandalwood and tea-root (a local plant), that balanced the odour of the hundred or so monks present at worship.

I remained with my brother. He blended in with the rest of his fellow monks, but his hair was wilder and shaggier than mine. He had a tonsure at the crown of his head. As the monks are devoted to God and God only, no one minded about one's look, *as long as he looked the part.*

Wilf was disciplined and fit to serve his upcoming priesthood at Totteringstate Parish Church. This will be a new step for him. After so many years cooped up at St. Gillacott's, Wilf looked forward to the change. I knew that a place like that would drive me mad, especially with the lack of the fairer sex. I also knew of the denials one had to make in order to enter. That was a sacrifice I could never make. *I had my weaknesses and my will would snap easily.* Boredom would set in and I feared I would become institutionalised. For a retreat, however, it was a welcome gift and a fine break from my reality.

In spite of my worldly preferences, I found it most wondrous, and a once in a lifetime journey to undertake such a measure and live in this manner.

The next day, after a good sleep, I awoke to the bell-chime of three. I got up with the others and Wilf to prepare for morning prayers.

When Matins concluded, we filed along the cloister to a large hall where a paltry breakfast was served, all in silence. *It drove me to despair not being able to speak to someone.* I always chatted with my friends and we would have lively conversations together. Here, though, the monks developed a way past the issue through sign language. I mused on the idea that it would be most fascinating to watch a pair of them having an argument using this methodology.

The hall itself was dismal, with grey coloured walls and a feeling of being further enclosed. It reminded me of something military or that of a residential school. Everyone sat at the long rectangular wooden table ready to eat. A further silence was observed for a quick gasp of prayer before eating. Then we all commenced on the diet of bread (lots of bread!), cheese, fresh fruit and ale. At other mealtimes, weekly or at a specific Feast, meat or fish was allowed.

As I ate, taking small bites and glancing 'round the place, I noticed a hanging at the far end of the hall. It was a tapestry in dedication to God's service, given to the monastery by my forebear, William. Wilf looked at me, smiling with a glint in his eye. This made him special to me and *I so wished he worked on the farm!* He made a sign at me, but I did not understand him. As a senior member of the Order, he had leave to whisper its cryptic meaning in my ear.

'How do you like it here so far? Please pass the salt,' he said.

I gave him a silent under-the-table thumbs-up, just revealing my hand for him to see. I then smiled back and served the request for the salt.

Knowing my knowledge of monk-signing was inferior, Wilf whispered again, 'Intense, isn't it?'

I gave him a stare and nodded.

The other monks continued to eat and stared at us in neutral. We felt like two naughty schoolboys messing about. Thankfully, our resemblances gave them the hint and it was understood. They also knew Wilf would be leaving soon, so they gave a kind, blind ear to it.

Once we had finished breakfast, we filed out to return to the sanctuary for more prayer and chanting... more prayer and chanting... *and on it went!*

Near mid-afternoon, a few monks had the happy privilege to copy manuscripts as part of a weekly task. I was one of the lucky few to work on a copy of a Book of Hours, where each hour of the day was allotted toward prayer and focus. It also had some intricate artistic detail, but I only concentrated on getting the words correct. (*The monks did not think a pig farmer would be artistically inclined.*) I was given a quill and parchment and told to copy as much as I could. An hourglass was set before me to ensure the other monks working on this project would contribute equally via fair rota.

Although I was taught to read and write, my recent livelihood did not involve creating calligraphic beauty. Doing accounts for the farm was most of my writing detail and I never gave it a second thought. However, I gave it my all and grabbed a quick minute of silence to get my mind focused. Once I turned the hourglass to the full side up position, I began the painstaking work, hoping I would not err.

A monk returned after an hour to see how I was doing. Knowing I was only there for a tick, he checked my work, but with leniency. He looked at what I *attempted*, as I tried to stifle emotional display. I was quite giddy inside and wanted to burst out with a raucous laugh. *The atmosphere here would suffocate the air itself!*

The monk had the parchment in hand, still verifying detail, nodded and smiled at me. He walked away and Wilf, waiting in the corridor, came to me.

'Catmartin liked your work. You seem to be a natural,' he whispered.

I stared back, and with my crack'd-pot version of signing, said, 'But I'm a pig farmer and have been far out of practice.'

Wilf continued, quietly, 'I know and understand you. God works through us and gives us the bridges to cross over when in adversity.'

I gave a face at him that closely resembled, 'Huh?' I then asked him if we can remove ourselves from these stifling premises where we could talk *alone*.

'There is a place where we could talk properly, far away from monks' ears. It is an advantage of being here many years. I go there for personal space and solitude when I wish to snatch a quick moment... others think I am in silent reflection outdoors and they are fine with it.'

Phew, I thought. We left the building and went to a nearby grotto across a small wooden bridge in the gardens. Our escape was complete and when we arrived, we sat on a rock and hugged each other intensely.

'It had been too long, brother,' I softly cried.

'Yea, it has, and I am impressed with your trying to fit in.'

'Thank you. I did hope my best was not put on trial here. God, I wish we could go to the tavern and have a drink together.'

'Not yet, my brother, not yet. Soon, I will bid farewell to this place and take up residence at Totteringstate Parish. I will get to see you more often and other than on Sundays. How do you like your retreat thus far?'

'Intense. If spiritual growth was measured in years, I feel elderly.'

'Indeed, that is the idea. The closer one is to God, the better.'

I loved God, but I did not want to get *that* close and confessed, 'I am truly not suited to the rigorous life here. I have my work on the farm, my friends, my Elizabethia...,' I sat in a trance just thinking about her.

'And how are your fellow farm colleagues?'

'Lively as ever.'

'I am happy to see you surrounded by your friends and it is good to be surrounded with purity.'

'For you, maybe. You do not know my friends,' I grinned.

'I was referring to the purity of friendship, brother,' Wilf explained.

'My love for Elizabethia should count, too,' I insisted.

'Yea, it does. When you decide to marry, I would be happy to conduct your wedding service.'

'Once we do marry, I am thinking of changing our family name too. I want to remove the damn'd stain from our existence.'

'Well, you are a peasant by punishment.'

'So are you, Wilf.'

'Ah, but I entered the monastery years before Father's fallout. I should not be counted.'

'You are still my closest family. I must correct this matter, and will so do. You'll see.'

'I heartily wish you luck on your effort,' he touched my sleeve, 'If it is all the same to you, I would be honoured to receive the new name, whatever you choose.'

'Thank you.'

We sat in silence for a moment, looking at a stone well in the middle of the garden.

'Have you told Thia of this?'

'No, I had not told her yet. I do not think she'd mind, however...man's priority, you know.'

'I can see where the arrow will point to upon your return home, brother. We must hurry, the next Mass will be starting.'

And so it went, for us to venture forth, in confidence and in love... *and more prayer!*

* * * * * *

My time with the Cluniacs had come to an end and I walked back toward Hastings Court. Wilf saw me to the toll bridge and wished me the best.

'I will send you news when I reach the Parish.'

'Much obliged, Wilf.' I gave him another hug.

'Look after yourself.'

''Til we meet again.' I turned to wave, as I saw Wilf walking away from the bridge toward to the sanctuary.

There was a flash of renewal inside me, as I walked my way back home. It was a long walk, but it cleared the head a bit and allowed me to think straight. The relief to see my friends and Thia was swelling like a levee about to burst.

CHAPTER XI

During my departure, Elizabethia had another liaison with Pym Sans-Brys. She was walking toward her place at Hastings Court where he eagerly spied upon her. From the time of the last meeting, Pym wanted the lass even more so. Once in view, Pym's eyes burst open with surprise and delight to see her again, but with the intention of taking her to his side. Cogs stirred awake and whirred in Pym's mind... *what to do now?*

He got off his horse, pushed decency aside and directed his attention to Elizabethia. A cruel smile emerged on his lips, 'Come ye here, if ye dare.' He continued bedding her with his eyes.

Elizabethia was confounded by the brashness of the man and the forwardness of his action. She knew he was a menace and the one who took her lover's former estate. *Why can't he go away and fight in a war, if that is what he liked?* She began to hate him, but he was a too titillating an appeal to resist and joined him. She lavished upon the whim, but was morally torn inside.

Yet, in a moment of over excitability, she came forward and reached for him in an embrace. Elizabethia's heart found itself sandwich'd betwixt two loves and desperately tried to find the way out. She felt helpless, in the power of his magnetism, and lingered a couple of seconds longer. She looked down and saw her chance to escape. Alas, she let that crazy emotion have its laugh elsewhere. She and Pym carried on intimately, with no escape for her.

They drew closer together and had stopped momentarily to look around, but did not care either way. They ripped themselves apart in sheer madness near a gooseberry bush.

The door to common sense flew wildly open, as her fingers fumbled into Pym's shift. 'Your ties are so very annoying. They are knotted in a way that one cannot go past,' she complained.

'Verily, my darling, you still must try,' he coaxed, 'Try anything, my child, by-the-by,' he lapsed into a relaxed posture, longing for the inevitable.

Frustrated, due to tiny hands and even shorter fingers damaged from a childhood accident, Elizabethia attempted the accursed knots, one by one... patiently... and with the loosening of the last tie, his whole world became undone. Pym sat there, in brilliant pasty coloured, alabaster white that gave way to a slight tanning during his travels. *Frankly, he was sexy... there was no doubt about that.* Elizabethia wanted to take advantage of this and enjoy the moment... *but she knew, deep down, she could not.*

Of course, Pym did not mind the ongoing attention and was more than happy to enjoy his forbidden fruit for now. As he was still unwed, this *was* forbidden, but he did not care. He was a warrior/philanderer and nothing more. And nothing more would please him than to take her back to Totteringstate Hall with the hope of soiling her within.

He bided his time carefully, eyeing her with a salacious stare. It was a stare that knew no bounds. She wanted to keep her honour clean, and would rather make him *think* he could take liberty. *Tempting him like this was delicious torture.*

He asked, 'So, where have you been all this while, my fair maiden?'

'Sir Pym, I am not your fair maiden,' Thia protested.

'Alas, I lack the space for a parcel like you in my bag, so I'd have you specially delivered,' he cooed, with bunny-eyes.

'To whom? To Roger?'

He scoffed and sniggered, 'No, my child, to my new home at Totteringstate.'

'You should not take what is not rightfully yours,' Thia insisted.

'Ah, but it is, my lady...if you *are* a lady. Remember my role at the estate. I was called in to mind the same.'

'For the now,' she snarled, 'I wish you would mind yer own business!'

The game between them was getting more daring. 'Oh, but if I could, if I could,' Pym tut-tutted, 'But then, whom have I to bear in such a place. I so long for it to be you.'

'I would bear a place only with Roger.'

His expression became downcast and he let out a sigh. 'Such is the punishment one must bear.'

'This is a small village, you know. People are talking and watching.'

'Let them watch,' Pym dismissed, waving his hand, 'I am Lord of the Manor. Those filthy peasants will do as I say.'

'Not for long. I know my Roger. He will return to his former status and he will be *your* Lord.'

Pym waved his finger at her, mocking her reference, 'Uh-uh-uh, only Christ is our Lord.'

Thia felt put out by that comment. 'Well, you know what I meant,' she spat.

'Indeed I do. Your intention is for me to bugger off and this estate become granted back to Roger. No, I will have it. You do me injustice, ma'am.'

'You, sir, *are* an injustice!' Her pouting continued.

'Look here, we can either argue endlessly, or we can enjoy our time together.'

'I cannot. I shall not fall.'

'By being with me, you have fallen,' Pym retorted.

'My word against yours and they know all about your devilish ways.'

'Perhaps I have treated you more than you deserve, like a lady... kind, yet fallible. Everyone's constantly at it, Thia.'

'But would I want to be?'

'Now, now,' he soothed, holding her close to his body, still. He turned her head toward his and began to kiss her. *Admittedly, this was enjoyable, but her will had to remain stronger.*

He continued, 'I want to tear down thy house and fly wildly into the bedroom where I can make sweet love to thee.'

Oh God! She had to think fast...

'Pym?'

He loosened his grip and answered, 'Yes?'

'I know of someone who will satisfy your every region,' she offered.

'Even the no-fair zone?'

'Especially the no-fair zone.' *Thia was loving this!*

He was intrigued from the start, 'Who is she?'

She was not going to let him off lightly. 'Oh, someone I know. A distant kinsman.'

'I do hope you meant kins*woman*.'

'Yea, whatever...kinswoman. But I will not tell you more until you and Roger sort out your differences. I know there is much tension betwixt you both.'

'Aye, that there is.' He got up and paced for a few moments. He glanced at her and made an odd, rash decision, 'Begone, fair maid, I let ye go. You just be sure to inform me of this kinswoman of yours, right? No funny business, eh?'

'You got it,' Thia shook hands with Pym and gave him a complimentary kiss, 'I won't let ye down. I will tell you this much, she is free, reasonable to look at and performs well. That is all.'

''Tis a most noble touch on your part, my dear. I thank you with the very life I were to give to your countenance.' He mounted his horse and turned toward Totteringstate.

Elizabethia waved at him, slightly cast adrift by his surprising comment. She thanked God for the quick flash of the inspiring idea. She made her way home to contact this kinswoman who lived in Leslington, in the northern part of Dumfushire.

* * * * * *

I must have walked a fair mile or so when I caught sight of Buckingham on a horse.

'Need a lift, Rog?'

I was none too pleased and climbed up behind him. It was a pinch at the best of times and it was far luckier still we could not afford a saddle.

Buckingham asked, 'So, how did it go with your brother?'

'Fine. He will be leaving the monastery soon to reside at Totteringstate Parish. He will be our priest there.'

'A priest? We could use a priest around here,' Buckingham scoffed, 'The one we've got is so old, he's been commonly mistaken for a pew... and he probably does!'

'Yea, but the wood shineth brighter,' I quipped.

We laughed for a bit, but it would mean a great deal to the Two Counties. The current fellow presiding had served nearly thirty years, give or take a minute, and a change was sorely needed. I am glad it was my brother...at least it was a comfort to know that one of my own would be back at Totteringstate itself, so close to our dear home.

'Cateliffe's filling the wagons for the pig's feed. He'll be meeting us to hitch it to this horse.'

'Whose turn is it to grain them?'

'Nay-Smith will have the pleasure,' Buckingham answered.

'That is good... I so miss Thia, and by all the saints, I shall have her; God, give me strength!'

Buckingham held silence which felt eerie.

I was unsettled and cried, 'What?'

'Sans-Brys had another go at her.'

My heart sank... and after all that I was planning, too. *No, no, not Thia!*

'I did not say she was *willing*, Rog,' Buckingham assured me, 'She might have given him something else, like...'

'Like what?' I demanded.

'Like a good hiding. I know she loves you and will be true to you. Sans-Brys is that devil in the grass, just waiting to take advantage of the moment.'

'Ummm....,' my mind tried to think of a firm solution.

I looked up and saw Cateliffe waiting for us by the side of the road with the grain. Buckingham slowed down and got off to help hitch the horse to the wagon.

'I'll carry on riding,' Buckingham offered, 'You can get in the wagon with Cateliffe.'

I jumped down and joined Cateliffe on the plank of wood at the head of the wagon, reserved for the driver.

Cateliffe began, 'You returned alright?'

'Yea, it was good to see Wilf again.'

'I heard he may be joining us shortly.'

'He begins his priestly stint at the church in Totteringstate in about a month.'

Cateliffe stared blankly at me for a second, 'I do not know how you did it.'

'Did what?'

'To conform to strict orders.'

'Well, it looks like we learn about one another daily, don't we,' I reflected, mimicking Wilf's line of thought.

'With your mind constantly on Elizabethia, I was doubting your sensibility.'

'Nah, I feel whole and refreshed.'

'You're not the only one,' Cateliffe commented.

'Oh?' I turned to him with suspicion.

'Did you hear about Sans-Brys?'

'Buckingham told me. Ol' Thia's got sense. She would never betray it.'

'Doesn't mean he wouldn't,' Cateliffe retorted.

'That wretch! He is constantly at it and we must put a stop to this nonsense.'

'We must get another girl involved. That way, Pym could get his own on *her* and leave your Thia alone,' he schemed.

Another girl, but whom??? My heart sank even further, for I did not know that many women, other than Pam-Anne and Elizabethia. We were a close knit group in work and in play and anyone else around us did not matter. The peasantry was put to work and dalliances were discouraged. Of course, it would not stop us from having a fling or two, but there needed to be a way out.

CHAPTER XII

Meanwhile, Elizabethia had written to her kinswoman and later told me of her meeting with Sans-Brys and the illustrious idea she had concerning him. I met with her to discuss the matter.

'Yea, Buckingham and Cateliffe heard you were with Pym and told me. It doesn't look good from here,' I warned.

'I was with him and will not deny it. He came upon me and had another go,' she admitted.

'Seems like he has taken a stunning shine to you, lass.'

Thia blushed. I wondered if it were possible to reconsider marriage with her, *but lo, I needed to be certain.* I gave her the chance to explain.

Firstly, I asked, 'Do you really love Pym enough for marriage?'

She was shocked at *my* forwardness, yet I demanded an answer. 'He is nice to look at and I would be surely dishonest with you if I told you otherwise. I have known you a long time, Roger, and I am happy to be your intended. Truthfully, I do prefer you over Pym. Pym has a dark streak in him and it makes me worried. Thou art light and my comfort is with thee.'

'Trying to be poetic, my Thia?'

'No, sir. I am trying to explain myself.'

'Really?' I gave her a smile and brought up a topic I previously discussed with Wilf. 'Listen, my lovely, once we are married, I want to change the family name.'

Her eyes widened. 'To what, sir?'

'I do not know. My brother Wilf had accepted whatever I choose for the name. I do not wish to begin our new lives together with a tarnished name. It has history, yes, but most recently, it has been quite unfavourable.'

'As I am marrying thee, Roger, I will accord to thy will,' she consented and mock- curtseyed.

'Oh, don't be like that,' I moaned.

'I was kidding around, Roger, but I am happy to be called to whatever you want to be called.'

I gave her a hug.

'Now, that you shared your idea with me, I have an idea that would rid that Sans-Brys from us, or at least me,' she continued.

'Oh? Cateliffe suggested a public *engagement*.'

'Good, because there is the upcoming springtime fete. You could compete with Pym in the sporting events. Winner gets the girl and all that.'

It was *all that* I was more concerned about... Totteringstate Hall... *and throw in the girl for good measure.*

'There is another scheme I have in mind,' she added.

My eyes widened. 'You? Oh, my dear, do tell!'

'Well, I sent dispatch to my kinswoman (who is a distant cousin) living in Leslington, northern Dumfushire. Her name is Matthia Quilliard.'

'Yes?' My interest in this had peaked rapidly.

'I told Pym I would introduce her and gave him the impression she was good enough for him.'

'Is she of his class?'

'Roger, he doesn't give a *damn* about class...as long as he gets whatever he wants. You should know what a snake he is, given that he is *your* kinsman!'

I did remember, but thankfully I hardly had any dealings with him until Father erred.

She continued, 'If he was keen on me, why wouldn't he be keen on her?'

'And why not?' I queried, 'Could it be that he wants to take everything away from *me?*'

'No, that is not it,' she turned away.

'What, then? How can ye be so sure?'

She turned to me, looking me straight in the eye. 'She is a bit subversive. I think Pym would appreciate a little risqué diversion.'

'How so?'

'This cousin of mine is actually called Matthias Quilliard, who has gender problems and thinks he is a girl; let us think of him as such.'

'Did you tell Sans-Brys about the subversion?'

She looked at me in a jovial manner and grinned, 'Would you?'

I let out a chuckle. 'Does 'she' work or have some kind of living?'

'Yes, she works at *The Incensed Rose* on a day shift and moonlights as a player with the Dumfushire Repertory. They plan to attend this fete and work with the troupe coming from abroad.'

'The local rep is a most suitable place for a chameleon.'

She laughed and hugged me, feeling things might work out after all. We decided to keep this to ourselves and planned not to tell the others, especially Sans-Brys, about cousin Matthia, or in reality, Matthias. *It would be crude justice, but the revelation would be priceless to witness.*

'If she is not of Pym's class, which coming from you, it sounds like she is not, then at least she could act it,' I stated.

'As long as she plays the part correctly, she could make Pym a less frustrated man. I sensed that in him. I can see why he is leeching upon my person.'

'Well, my girl, he shall leech no more. We have enough of the buggers to cure our ailments.'

'Problem is, he happens to be one,' she said.

* * * * *

It was early spring, nearing the time for the annual fete. It included many entertainments, dramatics, sport and other frivolities to make our world forget itself for awhile. A travelling troupe from Italy, in conjunction with the Dumfushire Repertory, was scheduled to perform for the fete, as Thia earlier stated.

Many a wedded match was created from the event and differences came to be settled (which became part of the sport). It fared as a renewal to all for both occasions.

I was in Totteringstate village, when I remembered what Cateliffe said to me about a public *engagement* against Sans-Brys. I headed to the local office that handled the sporting event. I spoke to the clerk, Callum Illiyard, regarding my small matter after introducing myself.

'Ah, what brings you here, sir?'

'I wanted to know if I could compete to show prowess against someone in particular.'

'I did not know pig farmers had any sporting prowess?!'

I blushed, but tried to ignore the comment. 'I do, and again, I wish to compete with someone with whom I have argument.'

'Who did you have in mind?'

'My cousin, Sir Pym Sans-Brys. There is issue between us that needs resolution and a reclaim toward my inheritance.'

'This is the same fellow who took over your former home of Totteringstate Hall?'

'The very same. How did ye know of this?'

'Word gets 'round in these small villages. Actually, I was expecting you to call,' Callum said.

'Oh?' I was surprised.

'I know you want to return to Totteringstate Hall, your rightful home, if it weren't for your father.'

I nodded, 'Yea, the Elderfynne affair.'

Callum smiled, as he checked some paperwork.

'So is it set?' The anticipation got the better of me.

'I can put you in for the archery and fencing competition. Winner claims the property of Totteringstate Hall. I have to make it personal, you see.'

'And the girl? Usually one gets the girl after combat,' I suggested.

'What girl might this be?'

'Elizabethia Woodes, my intended.'

'Yea, it is done.'

'Thia wrote to her cousin; we hope she will capture Sans-Brys and whisk *him* off his feet.'

'You are matchmaking for him?'

'It was Thia's idea. He's been making passes at her.'

'Disgusting brute,' Callum frowned, 'Why don't you marry her, then, if she is your intended?'

It had not occurred to me. *What was I waiting for?*

He continued, 'If you marry her now, the only thing you have to worry about is providing that sumptuous home of Totteringstate Hall for her. It could be secret; Sans-Brys needn't know until it is too late for him to retaliate.'

'Nice plan, but keeping secrets here is impossible,' I moaned.

'Suit yourself. Please sign here to confirm your intention,' he handed me a quill.

I signed the document and put sand on the ink for quick-dry purposes.

Callum reiterated, 'So, your matter will be settled by combat; winner gets the property in question. You already have the girl, because by then, you should be married to Thia. One less thing to fuss about.'

I cussed under my breath, as I became slightly anxious at the reality of my immediate action. But no matter; *he was right, by God!*

I turned to him, 'Thank ye Callum; my compliments to you and yours.' I shook hands with him.

'And the same to you Roger. Remember, get her whilst ye can.'

'Will do,' I acknowledged and left his office. I did not have many of *mine*, but my good friends will do.

Before going home, I stopped at a goldsmith's to purchase a ring for Thia. Once doing so, I turned and headed back to Dumfushire, as my business was concluded here.

I was still walking through the village when I ran into Wilset, who came over to greet me.

'Hello,' I called out.

'Ah, nice to see you, Rog,' he gave me a quick hug.

'What are you doing here?'

'Buckingham and Tarquinne dispatched me to the granary's supply shop. We need more grain for the pigs again.'

'We went through all that grain, already?!'

'Yea,' Wilset admitted, 'As well as the three compost heaps. Thankfully, we have spare and we're within the between feedings.'

God, those pigs are just that, pigs!

I asked, 'Can I offer my assistance to you?'

'We can head back together, you and I,' he accepted.

Wilset had a number of parcels ready to put on the cart. I helped load it for departure.

'Want to ride the horse, or on the driver's plank?

'I think we both should ride on the plank.' I felt it would be more comfortable after riding with Buckingham.

The horse was released from its post. Wilset carried the reigns into the cart and sat next to me.

We travelled through the village, as many of its inhabitants were preparing for the fete. Once past, we were met by Woolanshire's stunning countryside, and the other toll bridge that joined the Two Counties together.

Thankfully, this was not too close to Totteringstate Hall; the Hall itself was secluded by an overgrowth of vegetation and a path leading a mile or so into it. I breathed a sigh of relief once we passed the area. *I was in no mood for Sans-Brys right now.*

Wilset paid the pence into Dumfushire, and asked, 'You alright, Rog? You went all pale, just then.' He was concerned.

'I'm...I'm,' I stuttered, trying to get it out, 'I'm fine.'

'How now, then?'

'I've signed up to the sport event at the fete,' I glumly remarked, 'I am challenging Sans-Brys.'

Wilset looked aghast, 'He will whip you, you know.'

'No, he won't. And what's more, I will marry Elizabethia, post haste.'

He stopped the horse. 'No way, Rog!'

'Why not? What is the point of waiting?'

'I heard about her and Sans-Brys.'

'Forget about it, Wilset, 'tis old news. I am fully aware of it and spoke to her. She prefers myself to him.'

'Is that why ye challenge him?'

'Yea, and for the love of Totteringstate.'

'Your home,' Wilset reflected, 'Oh Roger, I wish you much luck. Hey, I know. Maybe we can help train you for this.'

'I would be honoured if you would all help. We must win back Totteringstate.'

'So you can live there again, but without us? After all the time we spent together,' he whinged.

'Totteringstate Hall is mine by right, regardless of what my father had done. I would need a home for Elizabethia, you know. A married man cannot live with his mates forever.'

He smiled and we rode on in silence. I guessed at what he wanted... a nice cosy place to live in, instead of the bunking up with everyone. *Tough shit, Wilset!*

The farm was nigh and I saw our staff in the distance, slugging it out in hard labour. *Well, in dealing with pigs and other sorts, it can be*; especially since we were to provide foodstuffs for the fete. The horse stopped by the barn and I helped Wilset unload the grain and put them on shelves inside.

I checked on the overall progress and was pleased. Everyone did their share and a message was waiting for me from my twin brother, Wilfin, saying he was now officially serving Totteringstate Parish.

Later, I penned a return message to him regarding my intention to marry Thia and challenge Sans-Brys. I sent Cateliffe to Totteringstate Parish to deliver it. Wilf also served St. Doublet in Dumfushire for early worship, but we usually attended there during periods of bad weather. There was a good following at St. Doublet's but we liked Totteringstate Parish more. It was bigger and where my family were all buried. It made me feel closer to my true roots as a Hastings. Now, I will match those roots to another and make my familial redemption come true.

CHAPTER XIII

A month later, after we gave time for the banns to be read aloud (thankfully without opposition from anyone... even Sans-Brys remained silent!), the union betwixt Elizabethia and I was held at St. Doublet. We would have loved to have had it at the larger Totteringstate Parish Church, but we did not want Sans-Brys around for the ceremony. My dearest had him wound up, but good, over a potential meeting with her cousin Matthia. *Eventually, the joke would be on him in the end, but it was too good a tension to dismiss.*

Whilst Wilf presided over the ceremony, my closest friends from Hastings Court were present as well as Thia's dad, who was proud to see his daughter *finally* marry into a thriving concern (i.e., our pig farm trade). It was a small do, where Elizabethia and I exchanged vows. We held the actual service inside due to intermittent rain that fell on the day. *I personally did not like doorstep marriages anyway... I wanted the fullness of the real thing.* Despite the vitality of our glorious moment, we felt like a multitude of fish in a compact basket. *Made it intimate, though...*

The time there was short and climaxed by my placing the ring I'd bought earlier, on her finger. We kissed to no end... *I was so grateful to have her and she had me.* Wilf was most happy for us and the final anticipation of the moment was but a glance in the past.

We kept to ourselves and hurried to Hastings Court, carefully dodging the rain. Most of us changed our tunics, for the mud upon them was unsightly. *It was a blessing that we decided to use the Chapel, thus, instead of the larger church.* Although Totteringstate Hall would have gladly housed many of us, Sans-Brys had his pride about him and wouldn't allow it. Actually, he did not care about anyone, other than what he can gain from them, in order to please his selfish desires.

The feast was held in our dining hall, where we normally eat anyway, but it was decorated with lavish finery, on the cheap (yet innovative). There was plenty of food, cooked by my fellow workers, Tudmond and Brackbury. Tarquinne went continuously to the market to buy extra things like other meat stuffs, offal, grains for bread, ready made cheese. We also feasted on a pig or two, which had grown up on our farm.

It was a close gathering and Wilf and Thia's father, Alfith had joined the merry band of my fellow farm workers/closest friends. As Thia and I were finally married, we would be able to share my room later.

We held a quick silence for Wilf's blessing our meal, when Thia's father shattered the holy moment like an anvil.

'Rog, I can get you and Thia a proper mattress for your room, if you like. Newlyweds don't shag on straw, especially if one of them is MY daughter,' Alfith offered.

'Why thank you, it would be most appreciated,' I smiled.

The others sniggered violently like schoolboys in a nunnery. I blushed and Thia kissed me.

'Blushing bride *and* groom,' Cateliffe guffawed.

'With curtains to match,' Buckingham quipped.

'And a horse to ride on,' Nay-Smith chided.

'Comfy saddle?' Wilset added.

'Is that all you lot think about? What about poor Pam-Anne, then?' I whinged.

'What about her? She's available and would take off,' Tudmond replied, giggling.

Pam-Anne sat in silence, eating, and stuck her tongue out at Tudmond.

A pause commenced. Then Alfith asked, 'Take off what?'

Tudmond did not hesitate, 'Well, you know….*whoosh!*' His grin stretched beyond the Two Counties. *He had the most ridiculous imagination!*

'You should stick to your farm work instead. Lofty ideals could mean trouble,' Brackbury concluded.

Tudmond sulked for a moment as our meal continued… *surprisingly, us peasants yearned for aspiration, even if it was just to climb the roof!*

Ah me... I looked at Wilf, who was slightly uneasy from the worldly chatter that was being cruelly flung around him. Alfith expected the naughty words, being once married himself.

We carried on into the night and the feeling went to more private thinking...

My lips bore fruit of vivacious being,
Thy laced-up mysteries contained within.
I bountifully sown a straw in your garden
And shall not gain from you, if I took it upon myself.
Thou wert a thrill above compassion,
A thrill beyond satisfaction...
My soul protrudeth into the bodice of your realm.
Upon a frame of speckled conscience, I gave it to thee...

Later on, Elizabethia, Wilf and I went on an excursion, by horse, to Totteringstate village. We had a discussion with the local magistrate, Wolfe-Harris, in respect to our name. Our father's infidelity put a shadow upon me that I had to shake off, if I were to have any future. He chose his life; he chose his woman... as did I... *but I did not want to be hindered by this.* It did not matter to Wilf either way, due to his clerical status, prior to the indiscretion.

I began the discussion, first introducing ourselves.

Wolfe-Harris noted the familiarity, taking a file off the shelf, 'Ah yes, Hastings,' he rustled out some paperwork, 'Descended from William Phillip de Hastings of Sur-Le-Merde, France?'

'Yea,' I answered, 'We want to change the family name.'

'Your father?' *It was obvious Wolfe-Harris knew about it, too... damn!*

'Yes,' I pouted, despite Wilf and Elizabethia's support, 'Any suggestions?'

Wolfe-Harris was in deep thought, flicking the quill on paper. The silence between us was deafening. If Wolfe-Harris could not come up with a solution, then I must plough forth with Hastings and let the memory pass with time.

The magistrate looked up and suggested, 'You could double barrel your names. It sounds better than you are, which, I reckon, is what you are after, and incorporating both names shows commitment betwixt you, Roger, and your wife. However, as you are the son of the fallen and your wife is of peasant stock anyway (and had not broken the law), *she* would have to take precedence.

'Your name, therefore, would be *Woodes-Hastings*. Does this sound appealing to you? It is not very offensive and your father's sin would not stick. *You can become your own ideal... and forge your own destiny*,' he concluded.

I gave the matter consideration and reflected... her name alongside mine... *Woodes-Hastings*. Now *that* sounded like a fine stroke. It didn't sound nasty... it wasn't a bad name. *Most unusual, certainly, under the circumstances....*

Elizabethia was chuffed to see *her* name listed before mine, but fully understood the situation and the magistrate's intention.

'I like it,' she said and looked at me.

'It's a start,' I relented, yet hopeful.

'I had agreed to the change too,' Wilf commented to the magistrate, 'I am Roger's only surviving direct relative and shall be called whatever he is called.'

'Splendid. If you sign your names, here, in agreement, your family name will henceforth be known as Woodes-Hastings, to take immediate effect. Now, how's that for a wedding present? And, as consented, Father Wilfin would also be given the new name.' Wolfe-Harris smiled with an eager eye.

Wilf was most pleased and thanked the magistrate with sincerity. I thanked him most humbly.

'Don't you lot slip up, now,' Wolfe-Harris warned, 'It is done in fairness and the family discretion will be forgotten over time.'

The prospect was boundless and, as a Woodes-Hastings, I was able to wipe the board clean, as they say, and begin afresh. I kissed Thia and gave brother Wilf a hug.

'I must return to the Parish, as there is work to be done,' Wilf said, 'I look forward to our Sabbath meeting.'

'Aye,' I replied excitedly, 'You are a most holy man and I feel contented by your service to us. I bet it feels good to use your voice again.'

'Well said, my brother. The feeling is most sublime. Now, I shall take leave.' Wilf turned to Thia, 'And you, good lady, welcome to our family and may thou fare thee well. The new name is most enchanting.'

'Thank'ee, Father,' she bowed.

Thia, you needn't do that!

Wilf got on his horse and set off toward the Parish.

Thia and I walked away from the magistrates building, daydreaming together along a busily occupied Wilset Green, when we saw a group by the tavern *The Wilset Green. The players!* I felt it was my big moment to meet them, as I, too, was an engaged participant in the fete. My pigs were well looked after by the farm staff, who I trusted well. *I have known them for years!*

'How about it Thia? Have ye a yearnin' to meet some foreign actors?'

'Go on,' she giggled, waving me on.

I went up to the larger, dark haired gentleman of the group... *this must be the leader.*

'Hello,' I greeted, clumsily.

'*Buongiorno*,' the man introduced himself, 'I am Alexi Razullo du Cleuxnz (still pronounced 'Kloonz'), impresario and manager of the *Gruppo di Arti Teatrali*.'

I sort of figured out what he said, but my head swam in a reverie of tree sap due to his heavy Continental accent. Thia approached by this time.

'You no speak?'

'I do apologise. I am Roger Woodes-Hastings,' I put my arm around Thia, 'And this is my wife, Elizabethia. We just married.'

'*Salute, facca bene*! You live here?'

'Next county over, in Dumfushire. I am originally from Woolanshire.'

'I see. I heard about a pig farmer in those parts... be you that person?'

'The very same. Your family name sounds familiar to me,' I suddenly recalled.

'Your name does too. I had a du Cleuxnz ancestor who travelled to England with someone called de Hastings during the Conquest. They went on a Crusade together.'

'I am his direct descendant, a few generations hence. He changed the family name to just Hastings and died on that Crusade, too.'

'Yes, that is correct and it was said that a dragon brought his remains to Totteringstate.'

I had heard about that too. The wonder of family history...

'I am descended from the third son (of the six children) my ancestor left behind during those days,' he added.

Soon, I was encompassed by du Cleuxnz, who had given me a bear hug. *Well, he was a big fellow!*

'Call me Alexi,' he invited.

'How did you end up in Italy?'

Alexi scoffed, ' Ah, it is a long story. People meet, people get ideas in their head and children come forth. My family's travelled around a bit and we met people who travelled around themselves. You know how it is.'

He definitely sounded like a world traveller (well, within the *known* world, anyway) and retained his Continental flair.

'We are staying at the tavern by this village green...ummm, *The Wilset Green*,' he said, trying to read the signage. He walked toward the group, 'Let me introduce you to my colleagues. This is Arturo DeMilo, Vesuvio, our mime, Viventi, Castilli, Silardicus, and Martynni, our playwright.'

'He writes all your plays?'

'Only the ones that had not been written yet that we can perform.'

'Sounds interesting,' I mused, 'By the way, how do you like England thus far?'

Alexi thought for a moment, 'The audiences are warm and the weather is cold.'

'Depends on the time of year.'

'True, but we manage. The village here is very hospitable. You said earlier you originated in this county.'

'I lived in Totteringstate Hall. My cousin was asked to take over the property due to...how should I put it, 'people meet, people get ideas and children are brought forth,'' I smiled at my attempt at paraphrasing the fellow.

Alexi laughed deeply, 'You have a good sense of meaning for a pig farmer.'

'I know and I plan to challenge my cousin for my former home during the sports trials.'

'Are you now? That would be most entertaining for us.'

'He's quite a good hand, Alexi, I could lose.'

'Nonsense! You are too clever. You are smart, like pig. You win.'

'There is another matter.'

'Yes?'

I exhaled, 'The repertory from Dumfushire will be joining you.'

'Good. The more, the merrier. Let them come. Now, we must set off. Martynni had written a new play for us and we need to rehearse it.'

I was intrigued, 'What's it called?'

'Una Casa da Dimenticare.'

I was speechless.

He smiled. 'Don't worry, it will be performed in English for your people. The title means '*A House to Forget*'. It is about a family quarrel.'

Sounds familiar, I thought. 'I understand. I do hope it gets well received here.'

'It had done well in other regions. It challenges the moral conscience.'

'Good luck with it and it was verily nice to meet you.'

We shook hands; he released his grip. 'I hope to meet you again.'

Thia and I walked away and left the players to their rehearsals.

CHAPTER XIV

We had a guest over at Hastings Court by the name of Yorkward Edfriar. He was called in to assist in my training at the fete against Sans-Brys. Although I already had prior experience with a sword, and bow and arrow, it was good to refresh my memory. It took me away from farm duties, but my staff made allowances for this. I was slowly becoming their leader, as such (since it was *my* family's business).

After a long day training, I was tired, but not tired enough to bed down. Buckingham, Tarquinne, Cateliffe, Nay-Smith, Tudmond, Wilset, Brackbury and I went to *The Incensed Rose* for a nightcap. Thia was tucked away in bed...snuggled under a warm duvet, atop her father's mattress, recently delivered with compliments. *It had made a most satisfying wedding present.*

We had a toast to us and our future and I announced, 'From henceforth on, we are to be known as Woodes-Hastings.'

Cateliffe made a face. '*Woodes*-Hastings?'

'Yes, Woodes-Hastings,' I said, with definition.

'What, all of us?' Tudmond asked.

I gave him a look. Tudmond smiled shyly.

Brackbury couldn't resist, 'Shouldn't it be Hastings-Woodes?'

'We discussed the matter with Wolfe-Harris, the magistrate, and he suggested the name,' I explained.

'Ah, makes it legal, then,' Nay-Smith commented.

'How so?' Buckingham frowned.

'Because she takes priority over me,' I reminded him, 'Remember the sin of my father.'

Buckingham thought a moment, looked at Tarquinne, who rolled his eyes, and a spark of recognition sprang alight in Buckingham's head.

'Right,' he nodded.

'Anyway, I can put us in better footing, with your help and we can re-brand ourselves and start anew,' I suggested.

Tudmond chimed in, 'Does that include us?'

'Yes. Not just Thia and I, but all of you, too and the farm will still continue as is. We are running it well, are we not?'

'That we are,' Wilset agreed.

'And I intend to reclaim Totteringstate Hall,' I spoke hopefully.

Some of them looked up at me. 'Cateliffe, Nay-Smith and Wilset already know of it,' I continued.

The group looked at them and Wilset, who was certain I would lose, stood his ground, 'He's going to beat you; remember, he's a soldier.'

'That doesn't mean anything,' I exclaimed, 'With Edfriar's refreshing my memory of earlier training, I intend to win.'

'I wish ye luck and good fortune,' said Cateliffe, 'Or you and your good lady will be with us at Hastings Court for some time.'

'Nah, that won't happen,' I assured him.

I surely prayed my optimism remained steadfast... *I cannot let that bastard win!*

* * * * * *

In the fullness of spring and after the Easter feast, the day of our Fete arrived. It was held on a weekend, when the world suddenly grew busier than ever. There were some stalls set up at Wilset Green, akin to the Market, mostly selling foodstuffs as well as representatives from local charities asking kindly for donations. *The Wilset Green* (renamed a couple of hundred years ago due to an accident most incendiary) was filled to capacity and many of the locals had used their houses to accommodate the incoming visitors. Totteringstate Hall would have been perfect for a great many of our guests, but Sans-Brys wouldn't entertain the like. He liked his privacy and demanded solitude, unless it were a woman...*then, he would entertain.*

We had a stall on the Green and due to my colleagues' originality in selling other items from our farm (such as that bathing product we had discussed earlier and the lard which could be used for other purposes), we did well for ourselves. The scents and oils to make the bars smell pleasant were sourced from a local herbalist, in exchange for our meats. It was ideal for us and some other stall holders considering many people attending came for our local delicacies... *and it was most thoughtful of them to include us.*

From everywhere, people gathered to take part and enjoy the festivities from our counties of Woolanshire and Dumfushire, some all the way from London and others, even further, in the case of Alexi's Italian players group, who came specifically for the event. They had their mime and mummery acts catering for children and they also joined with the Dumfushire Repertory for the more serious play. The one Alexi informed me about when I first met him, *A House to Forget*, was billed for the afternoon.

I helped out at our stall for the morning on the first day, then I attended to further last minute training with Edfriar for the sporting event to be held in the nearby hamlet of Silarby (due to the vast expanse which was ideal for these tournaments). The scary bit was it was to be held on the morrow. Yet, I held no fear and knew my ground. I just could not wait to reclaim my ground of my home at Totteringstate Hall.

Meanwhile, the children's performance acts were winding down and after the lunch break, everyone gathered to see the new play. There was anticipation in the air, especially that Thia's cousin, Matthia, was to play the lead. It intrigued me, as Alexi pointed out that it 'challenged the moral conscience'. As that is all I knew about it, I let my judgement pass until I was more familiar with its scenario. Of course, no storyteller would allow himself to give the game away, and this was no exception. Everyone looked around with baited breath, as word of this play supported positive movement.

I got together with my closest friends, Buckingham, Nay-Smith and Cateliffe and left Wilset, Brackbury, Tarquinne and Tudmond back at the stall. My wife Elizabethia and brother Wilfin had joined us too. Wilf was not a theatre goer, obviously, but chose to indulge this once, strictly for religious and observational purposes only. I reckoned if this play dealt with morality issues, it may interest him; *otherwise he had no sense of theatre!*

Luckily, Buckingham brought along some snacks prepared by Pam-Anne back home and we all tucked into what looked like biscuits and some fruit. We found them delicious and the fruit was refreshing for early spring. The use of the lard made the biscuit treat tastier.

At the sounding of two bells of the afternoon (to indicate the hour), the Players assembled to begin the performance. All who were gathered, which were a great many, had quieted down and the Chorus went...

A House to Forget?
A Questionable Upbringing!
To take a Child of Christendom
And falsely raise it Another Way?
And what is The Way, pray tell?
The Way it was, The Way it is;
Withal!
It is uncovered village green
Growing upon lands, unseen;
To devour all victims within,
And to force them throw away a piece of themselves in contempt.
Herein, The Way is like wasted matter, transformed...
You cannot get away from it...
And it is still shit.

The play went on for a bit and I saw what Alexi meant by his
challenge of the *moral conscience*... these were some selections:

The lead, now known to us as 'Macchia' spoke her ditty, crying out
to God:

Exhume the monotony from my eyes
For my soul's conscience, shall I weep?
For a plate of stew, doth life deprive a hungry soul?
For a frame of being, hath not words mark an angry toll?
Upon my speckled conscience, I give myself to Thee.
Like a cold brooding silence, I stand in the rain,
Awaiting Thee.

The wicked Grandmother held an unyielding card, as well noted:

'Ye are of The Way,
In The Way
and By The Way...
There is no escape from The Way.'

It turned out Macchia was adopted by grandparents who were not Christian and falsely claimed their devotion to *The Way*. Macchia's father, a Roman soldier and a Christian, was ousted out of taking care of his own daughter by the mother's evil parents. The mother had since died shortly thereafter. Taking the chance in having Macchia baptised (hoping the mother's family would not find out and that it would bring the child closer to God), he fled to his Regiment, leaving her with the mother's family, *regrettably*. It was apparent that they did not take proper care of the child, for there was much ado regarding this arrangement. The tirades were admittedly difficult to believe. What was worse for that family was they did not admit to *their* fault and apologise, for they misrepresented themselves and forced *The Way* unto an un-blighted soul. Macchia becomes tarnished with the memory and stigma of falseness; however, her cries to God do not go unnoticed. He saw the intense distress, and in His Son, she was healed throughout.

There was a mighty cheer when the actor, DeMilo, playing Christ, appeared to Macchia, who gave her much comfort:

'I support thee, my daughter,
For I can see thee duly sanctioned;
Not owing to fault,
For thy Love of Me.
I can see the grave Mistake made,
Nothing personal unto thee.
I will send thee hence to thy Rightful father,
To a place where the past shall nay run free.'

The Roman soldier-father was played by Alexi himself (in a mask). He was very imposing on stage:

'I am your Celebrated Father, Macchia. I have come to take you home.'

Macchia responded:

'Oh, the falsehood of religion,
Betrayed by my former hosts,
Who once called themselves...
Family!
I must get a Divorce,
And rid myself of The Way.
Oh, unquiet heyday of childhood,
Disruptive tantrums in the night;
Will it be more frightful with solitude
Or familial strife?'

I thought that Thia's cousin, Matthia, was superb in her portrayal of the heroine, Macchia. The final scenes showed Macchia's return to Italy, where she lived with her father, along with the rest of his family. The father continued his stint as a soldier, and Macchia helped out in picking grapes at the vineyard and studying Classical literature to cleanse her mind from *The Way*.

The 'Christ' character saw that all was not lost, and ascended into Heaven, feeling His job well done. The mother's family was then excommunicated from their respective community and barred from ever pursuing *The Way*. They were also further punished by God Himself for messing with an innocent.

There was thunderous applause, along with a standing ovation for the play and we all cheered for Alexi and his group. Matthia received a bouquet of flowers to commemorate a successful performance. I looked at Thia and asked her if we could go meet with Alexi again to congratulate him and to share our thoughts on the play. She agreed and we left to do so. Buckingham and the rest returned to the stall, finishing up another good selling day.

CHAPTER XV

Thia and I headed for the players group, when we met up with Sheriff DeMoro. I told Thia to go find Alexi.

'Good show,' the Sheriff said, 'A most unusual story.'

'It was an original play, written in-house,' I replied.

'In-house?'

'I met the group and one of them is a playwright.'

'Handy to have accessible, I suppose.'

'The more original, the better.'

'Yes, well,' DeMoro rubbed his chin, 'I have news for you regarding that market incident.'

'Which one?'

'The one where a thieving wench used a child to target your missus.'

My eyebrows furrowed. 'And?'

'It turned out they were foreigners and returned to their own country. Due to boat conditions, both mother and child died en route. You needn't worry about them.'

'What about Maisel?

'Oh, her,' the Sheriff grinned, 'She's been with me since that Market day. After she helped you with your stall, I took her in myself. I did not think farm work would be suitable for her, and with all you men surrounding her, well.'

'She is quite young, but not that young. She's in that tricky phase.'

'Yes, and with all you lot cracking male-filled jokes about,' he gazed heavily at me.

'I understand. A great many of them are like that.' I felt sheepish and hated to admit that my friends *lacked* women.

'The grandmother herself was questioned in custody, but never gave us a straight answer. It was as frustrating as shooting an arrow that misses its target. Still, she was quietly dealt with. 'Tis of no further concern. There had been enough incidents for more than my liking and morality lessons are the last thing we need.

There was a pause. 'Don't let me keep you. I am sure there are many folk here who need keeping in order.'

'Quite. I dislike these *want-for-it* events; alas, that is where I earn my shilling.'

'Indeed, it doth,' I stuck out my hand.

'Good day to thee,' the Sheriff shook my hand and left.

Thia came to me with Alexi.

'Roger,' he beamed.

We exchanged hugs.

I blurted, 'What inspired you to write such a story??'

'Martynni gets his ideas from many places but there is a *Legend of the Screaming Chiazza*, which is the topic we portrayed. It is a harrowing story; we put Christ in it to give full effect.'

I asked, 'Was the legend real?'

'Yes, but it happened so long ago, and most people don't remember the details. However, we did not want to call the heroine 'Chiazza', so we used a different name, which served the purpose,' Alexi explained.

'Matthia was fantastic,' Thia commented, 'I liked the play overall, very imaginative.'

'Martynni has an excellent imagination which is why we use his work in our repertoire.'

I looked at Alexi, 'You will be returning to Italy soon.'

'Not yet. We have some dates in the West counties and depart from the Cornish coast back home.'

'I was so privileged to meet you. I do hope you stay, as you know I am in a performance,' I said.

'For you, I stay. I am not into sport, but I do approve of fighting for honour.'

'As honourable as *A House To Forget*?'

Alexi laughed, 'I remembered you stating you were going after your cousin to restore the family reputation.'

I smiled, 'That is right. It will be in the hamlet of Silarby, as the fields there are far wider than here in Totteringstate.'

'We look forward to it. Good luck and *auguri*.'

I gave him a blank stare.

'Best wishes, my friend.'

I sighed with relief. 'On the morrow, at ten.'

'I want to see you win back your estate.

'I thank thee, most heartily.'

We exchanged hugs again and departed where Thia awaited me. No sooner we walked away from the players' group did Sir Pym Sans-Brys turn up... *we expected this*. Thia and I both knew he was eager to meet Matthia, who was staying amongst her colleagues and their foreign counterparts. I reckoned this was a good time for them to meet anyway, *for better or worse*.

'Good morrow, my lady,' Sans-Brys greeted, mockingly as usual.

'Sir Pym,' I shook hands with him, ''Tis good to see you on such a fine day.'

His tone became aggressive, 'Never mind your pleasantries, pig farmer, where is that saucy-sue I saw on the stage??!'

My, my, did he have a way with words...

'You are quick, straight to point and as sharp as an arrow,' I complimented him.

'You know what I am here for,' his eye caught the glimmer of gold on Thia's finger.

I looked at Thia and indicated her to fetch out the desired prize and then tried delay tactics, 'That play we saw was enduring.'

'It was silly and full of wistful nonsense,' Sans-Brys spoke, with a soldier's un-sentimentality, 'I just want to see the girl!'

His stance was like a bull, baying for the attacker's blood. He looked tragic, sort of desperate, possibly pathetic. Ornate, but only as a facade... there was nothing beneath. *He was only a soldier. He would not understand the finer things of life.* Pym's time of soldiering overran his pursuit of the fine arts.

'You don't mince words,' I replied.

'Ye don't hold your action either. I saw the ring. You now married?'

'Yes, we did marry and changed our familial name.'

'Won't change your status, though; you are still piss-lined peasants. Now, you have kept me here for some time, where is this Matthia???'

Thia broke the stale air, which emerged betwixt Sans-Brys and myself, accompanied by Matthia, who was much in desire at the moment.

Thia gave me a kiss, went up to Sans-Brys, and said, 'Behold, your Matthia.'

'Mat--h--i--aa??' He began to stutter. The lovely image he built up in his mind had been winding therein so delicately and torturously. *Now that he saw Matthia, well....*

Matthia was tall, just under six foot. Wearing a plain dress, no makeup, but the face looked...*male* and she wore spectacles--thick framed... especially imported from abroad. The male face was comely, but with the out-of-place apparel beneath, the sight had shocked Sir Pym out of his mind.

The frustration built up inside him had swelled beyond that of a volcano... *there wouldn't be enough land to fill up the outcast-ed detritus with!*

Matthia read the signs...and understood. She explained, 'Everyone reacts to me like that. 'Tis of no matter to me,' she paused, then continued, 'My name is actually Matthias. I wanted to go a-stage and be a player. I also had a fancy toward women, but not in the same sense you would see it as. I wanted to be one, you see, and this seemed to be the perfect medium in which to fulfil that yearning. I even get to work as a bar-wench too. None of the men want to do the girl's roles, and I am more than pleased to perform. Convenient, eh?'

Sans-Brys nearly hyperventilated; his ever-so-glamorous balloon had popped out of existence, and a wave of change came over him. It was not in his character to change, but, *even the best of us can move a mountain toward change.*

He said to me, apologetically, 'I didn't mean to be so harsh on you or your lady. It is difficult to have what you want and have nothing.'

'I know it too well, Sir Pym, I work with a great many that think like you do,' I reflected, thinking about Buckingham, Cateliffe, Tudmond and the rest back at the farm.

'You needn't take that sore sentiment with me... you peasants never had it good,' he spat, 'How would you know what you're missing?'

Oh, I knew what my lot were missing, but remained silent about it. 'I had it good once. I will have it good again...after I challenge thee!'

He smiled, 'Perhaps...maybe...but if you shew too much eagerness, ye'll step into an abyss of it.'

'I may step into an abyss and fall in, but nay like my father,' I argued.

'Don't press your luck, farmer; th'morrow will hasten decision,' Sans-Brys snapped, regaining the more familiar character that he was.

'Th'morrow at ten will settle both our futures,' I cried out.

I breathed a sigh of relief when I saw him walk away from us. Matthia was unconcerned regarding Pym's behaviour, as she explained earlier, but led us to a bench and treated us to drinks from an outdoor vendor.

'I did tell Pym you were an actress… well, sort of,' Thia blushed.

'I am sure you did, dear,' Matthia cooed, 'By the way, what did you think of the play?'

Thia and I looked at one another, trying to reckon an answer.

'Your performance was impeccable and fascinating,' Thia tried it on first.

I held her statement, 'The story was most unusual and refreshing to us provincials.'

'Yes, it would be to most provincials,' Matthia agreed, 'I heard those in London were too familiar with that scenario, due to some living there that do not practice Christianity.'

'Ah, I see,' I smiled, sipping my ale, 'I am sorry it did not go right with Sans-Brys.'

'Oh pooh, Sans-Brys,' Matthia dismissed with a wave, 'I know his type and I am not cosy to a soldier's mind-set or attitude. They may sneer at people like us; yet, the world does not forget its many vices and plagues of our society such as war, illness and hunger.

'We use our talent to work toward a purpose for the community that needs to forget itself, but for a quick while. The world would be in a finer mess than it already is. I do not want to be responsible for an unhappy world. We, as players, respond to its call to heal through entertainment. This is so important...even if one has to go through lengths to further one's skirt.'

'I see,' Thia giggled.

I understood the message, *but obviously could not relate.*

'Even the Church is kind to us,' Matthia added, 'Some of our takings are donated by our Repertory toward charity.'

'I find it odd that they don't see you as a witch,' I commented, 'With your dressing habits and the like.'

'Everyone here knows me. Perhaps if I travelled, things could get tricky, so I would not go there.'

'I wish you much success,' I got up to hug Matthia, 'Even if you are off your rocker.'

'Thank you,' Matthia embraced me, 'I heard you'd married,' she added.

'We wanted it private.'

'Yea, I would hate to have put a damp rain patch on your affair,' Matthia lamented.

'You wouldn't have. St Doublet's is a small button of a church,' I reassured, 'But most welcoming to all.'

'Chapels are known to be well-confined,' Thia chimed thoughtfully.

'Yea, well, cheerio. Godspeed to you both,' Matthia called out, walking back to *The Wilset Green* to rejoin her group.

I started to giggle myself and told Thia, 'What a card you have for a cousin.'

'Takes all sorts, don't it?'

'I suppose so,' my words trailed past a tourist group to find Sans-Brys fully recovered from his time with us and happily conversing with two women... *or was that a mother and daughter?*

We approached, out of curiosity, when the older woman saw us and introduced herself, in a very heavy accent that rivalled Alexi's, 'I am Descaria Barbellicos and this is my daughter, Cyndosia, who is chatting with a very nice young man.'

Cyndosia looked up and waved, then returned to her *very nice young man... Sans-Brys!*

I composed myself, 'I am Roger Woodes-Hastings and this is my wife, Elizabethia.'

'Ah, charmed to meet you.'

I wondered, 'Your name sounds Greek, am I correct?'

'I came over with Alexi and his players group. I am his godmother. We go back, long time. We know each other and seek a match for my daughter.'

'Husband-hunting, eh?'

Mrs Barbellicos laughed, 'Go on, you amuse me.'

I got a good shot of her and thought she looked well-aged, trying to be pretty, *but we all know she's past it!* Her dark, rich brown hair was piled, complicatedly I presumed, inside her silken peach coloured headdress. The clothes were...um...not something I would wear travelling... even if *I* dressed en femme, like Matthia. The daughter, well, well, well. She was a looker. My mind made rude whistling noises thinking about her, but I contained myself accordingly (*in attempt to recall that day at St Doublet's*).

Cyndosia was of small stature, forever-youthful looks (could pass for 25, though I did not press to query), long golden blonde hair wrapped around her head in an exquisite pattern, pleasing face, expressive brown eyes... *I could see Pym's interest in her.* Although she was an excellent distraction, I was more keen to see how Pym was getting on. I smiled to myself, just watching them.

Cyndosia broke the inner realm with her interruption. 'Mama, Sir Pym invited us to visit Totteringstate. Can we go, favore, favore?'

Mrs Barbellicos conceded, 'Si, si, certo. You may go.' She turned to me, 'I am intrigued by this Totteringstate.'

'It's only a Hall,' I spoke sharply, thinking of the bare cheek of it all. And it figured that Sans-Brys had *intentions*... he tried wooing my now-wife, and now to plan wooing this foreign girl... *in my house... my house!!*

Thia, meanwhile, went on a mercy mission on my behalf and it turned out to be to our advantage, though the effect on Sans-Brys was a bit inconvenient. She went to Alexi and informed him of what happened between Sans-Brys and her cousin, Matthia. Alexi was privy to my challenge with Sans-Brys over my family home and honour. So, having his godmother and her daughter travelling with his group to find the daughter a husband, put Sans-Brys in a potentially vulnerable position.

We all knew he was a sucker for women, his appetite so insatiable, it would take a huge serf-force to create an item to make him happy. The meeting with Sans-Brys and Cyndosia was thus arranged; *perhaps he will piss away from Thia and have a new toy to play with.* Maybe this new girl could tame his wild nature and cool down his appetite for fighting. *I personally never liked fighting, myself.*

Mrs Barbellicos asked me, 'You go Totteringstate?'

'No, no, but ye go on. It is lovely there,' I lamely encouraged.

'You sound sad,' she noticed.

I had to admit it. 'It used to be my family home.'

'Ah, Sans-Brys mentioned someone named Hastings or something,' Mrs Barbellicos realised. 'There is a pig farmer from Dumshire, or something like that, called Hastings...is that you?'

'Yes; the family name was changed and the county name is Dumfushire,' I corrected.

'Why Dumfushire?'

'Local legend; long story.'

The mother quickly changed subject. 'What you think of my daughter?'

'Beautiful. Distracting.'

'She's a throwback with that blonde hair.'

I gave the lady a look.

'Well, we're all dark haired in the family, to my knowledge. I came from Italy, married a rich Greek merchant. When he died, he left me everything. So, I come to England with Alexi to find nice man for Cyndosia.'

'You think Sans-Brys is it?'

'I *know* he is,' she poked my chest with her lavishly bejewelled finger.

'I am to challenge him. He is my cousin. He took over Totteringstate when my family... umm, that too is a long story.'

'You seek correction from this?'

'Aye.'

'You do good. I see that my daughter treats your cousin... *well*,' Mrs Barbellicos winked.

'Keep him occupied. Good to meet ye,' I bade farewell.

'Much luck to you,' she answered back, waving.

I was now wondering where Thia was. Ah, there, with the players again. I went to join them and relaxed amongst the merriment.

CHAPTER XVI

The hamlet of Silarby was used for military practice since the Conquest. It was lush green land with a few houses nearby, used for storage purposes. It lent itself well to accommodating an assault course and had room for methods of skill like sword fighting and archery. There was the occasional jousting match as well, a big-leaguer's game, where muscle had to match equally with armour, colliding with the inevitability of speed.

Silarby was used for the day's sporting challenges, in which I am participating against Sans-Brys. It was useful, like the jousts, for competitors to show off their abilities. Some of the games were proven deadly; death, in my opinion, was too good for Sans-Brys. *Fate shall determine this*, and I left it at that.

My thoughts were further a-field when I received a private message from Sans-Brys to meet with him before the challenge. The message *cryptically* stated he wanted to get this event over and done with and had no further interest in shaming me any longer. I wondered what had gotten into him.... *probably that foreign girl*, I chuckled. I folded the paper away into my tunic and mounted my horse for the wee hamlet.

Setting off early, I rode my horse, accompanied by Cateliffe and Nay-Smith, who were there as seconds, as well as for my morale. Thankfully, my armour was waiting for me at Silarby, which was seen to by Buckingham and Wilset.

Cateliffe recognised my far-away look. 'You be careful, Rog, I know you are nervous about this. Mind your hooves.'

'Stop babying me, Cateliffe, I do know how to ride, thank you,' I retorted.

'He's only watching out for you, mate,' Nay-Smith interjected, 'No need to get so touchy.'

Cateliffe followed on, 'We are trying to secure our place with you, whatever that is worth!'

'It's only a game,' I sighed.

Cateliffe and Nay-Smith stopped their horses, surrounding me. I looked surprised at them and urged them to move along.

'It's not a game, Roger Alexander Woodes-Hastings,' Cateliffe chided, as a parent would, 'This is honour... *your family honour.* You've just gotten married, changed your surname, making us believe in the new brand. Don't accurse your new name by being smug and dismissive. You'll be as bad as your father...worse even. Your stain will afresh the locals of your father's past. Our business will be ruined. *You will screw us all if you mess this up!'*

The fellow had a point, and it hurt.

Nay-Smith came up to me, 'This event will decide all our futures. Just remember who you are *now* responsible for.'

A pause befell us... *Thia?*

We rode on, with only myself knowing the *possibility* of Sans-Brys throwing the match in my favour and splitting away with that girl. Of course, I wouldn't tell my mates about his earlier message to me. I knew they meant well and had their interests vested in me. Our farm was our life and livelihood and I could not let anyone down now. I still needed to meet with Sans-Brys, as requested... *but where, when?*

'You two go on to Silarby, I will meet you later,' I hastily led my horse toward Totteringstate Hall.

Cateliffe and Nay-Smith looked at each other dumbfounded, and carried on to Silarby.

I knew I was riding into 'enemy' territory, and the Sans-Brys touch had not gone unnoticed in the paths leading up to the grand Hall. Overgrown hedges made excellent breeding grounds for bandits and other loose rogues in the area; uneven grounds made the equestrian ride slightly clumsier; odd smells needed to be dealt with. *Once I regained Totteringstate, I shall correct all this.*

It must have been such a party the previous night. The amount of strangers in my old household disgusted me. I wondered if he reconsidered our match... *I had to get to the bottom of it.*

Upon seeing the familiar edifice, there was certain bustling inside. The windows remained, as they were in my day. There were flags and heraldic shields lined along the outer wall of the house, showing intention and corresponding pomp.

Nervously, I dismounted from my horse and waited by one of the overgrown hedges. I watched as carefully as I could. I saw Sans-Brys come out, looking absolutely flash in his red velvet cape, a fawn coloured tunic, studded with silver buttons at the edges, and showing his insignia against a black breast-plate, grey coloured hosiery and riding boots. His blonde hair glistened in the sun, and, *if I were a lady, my God, would I faint at the sight!* As I am a man, my stomach flipped over in hysterical strain. I reckoned he had his second ready his armour at the field, as I did.

'Hand me my pole, serf,' he shouted out to his servant, who did as duly instructed.

Sans-Brys re-entered the Hall. *Always trying to be the big hand...*

I wondered if I had gone too far in doing this. *Should I go and speak to him?* Maybe our differences could be resolved here once and for all and to hell with the Silarby challenge. But there were paying people waiting... *I could not let them down.*

A rash decision was made and I raced to my mount. I rode my horse on, hard and fast, before Sans-Brys, or anyone else, had a chance to spot me. Our moment to speak will have to wait.

Silarby was another mile when I saw crowds piling through to take their seats. Scores of people loved to see these events and attended them annually. It was their only source of *rough* entertainment. Those who went to the theatre to watch oddball folk like Matthia take their stance, were looked on as milksops by comparison.

I frantically tried to locate Cateliffe and Nay-Smith. Upon my horse, I was thankfully spotted and Cateliffe ran over to take my reins to the arena. His pull was so sudden, I nearly toppled from my horse.

'Where were you? You need to be in battle dress now. They've started the first event already,' Cateliffe scolded.

'Aye, and I apologise deeply.' I felt sore, getting down from the horse.

'Go to Nay-Smith, he will see to it,' he instructed.

I felt like a naughty schoolboy again...only I was alone. *No twin brother this time.*

Nay-Smith grabbed me and started putting on my assigned armour. 'This is your big chance. You have much to live up to and think of the people who have helped you over the years. The farm! Elizabethia!' He spoke to me like an inner conscience.

Inner conscience or not, I knew what I had to live up to, and *who* I needed to knock down in order to do it.

Buckingham, Wilset, Tudmond and Tarquinne turned up to wish me luck.

'We will be watching you, Rog. Please don't over do it, you know what Sans-Brys is like,' Buckingham reminded.

I knew what the man's like; what's his game, now, anyway? Where the heck is he?

Thia and Wilf came up to me with familial love and well-wishes.

'Go get th'bastard, brother,' Wilf said, totally out of character.

'Wilf!' I exclaimed, hardly believing my senses. *Was this the same person I met during my monastic respite?*

Thia interrupted, 'Don't worry...it's his hot-spur of the moment. Isn't it, Wilf?'

The priest smiled. *That brother of mine.... oooh!*

They parted company and no sooner from the time they left me, Sans-Brys turned up, wearing his even flashier armour. He looked astounding in breath-taking black coloured metal, with gold motifs depicting botanical and faunal motifs.

A loud cheer was heard as a wrestling match commenced, which heralded the crowd's recent display of excitement.

Sans-Brys asked, 'You sure you want to go through with this, Hastings?'

'It is Woodes-Hastings now, and I am prepared to undergo our promised challenge,' I answered.

'Well, I shew good intention by my attendance, but as I stated in the note to you, I no longer want your measly estate, nor have I any interest in furthering the shame on your family... *even if you did change your name*. I wish to concede to you.'

Was I hearing him correctly? 'There are people who travelled far to see this and the locals, well, if they hear about it...'

Sans-Brys interjected, begging, 'No, no, wait... Let's, let's not say any more. We will give them a good show. I will allow you to do me justice. Let me live and I will exit your life and England forever.'

'WHAT?' I was astonished.

'I found a better path in life, a better way and a more gentler system.'

Was this the same Sans-Brys we all loved to hate?

'You? No way. You will not get out of this one, Pym!' I had no care to address at this time.

'I am in love. Love, with the most beautiful, available girl e'er put on this planet. I must have her. A volcano's fury doth not match the feelings I had upon meeting such a luscious entity.'

I was sceptical. I folded my arms and asked, 'Who is it this time?'

'Cyndosia Barbellicos.'

'You are throwing away your oath as a soldier and every belligerent stance you took upon me for *that girl*???'

'Yes,' he said, starry eyed by this point. His gaze looked most peculiar, staring out into the distance, as a lost poet would.

'We cannot throw the match,' I argued, ''Twould be unfair.'

'Do it for my sake, Roger Woodes, or whatever you call yourself now. Please, for old times sake,' he still begged (*pathetically, I might add*).

His eyes looked different. They were in an apologetic, desperate, wishing-to-forgive mode.

'We cannot end this here. Our challenge must go on,' I demanded, feeling a tinge of suspicion.

'Alas, I cannot go on,' Pym sighed wistfully, looking distant and as wet as a damp cloth. *This wasn't like him.*

Nay-Smith and Cateliffe came in aggressively, 'What the hell do you two think you're doing, you both are up next,' they shouted.

Pym stared at the men, no longer that steaming soldier he once was. *This Cyndosia better be worth it.*

Cateliffe panicked, 'Is he whacked?'

Nay-Smith responded, eyes fixated upon Pym and I, 'I don't know, but if there is something going on betwixt you, do it outside and serve the paying public!'

I overheard the next bell, tolling for our blood. It was our turn and *there was no backing out now.*

'Pym, if anything happens, I will ensure you live... even if I have to wound you a bit,' I assured.

'Thanks Roger,' Pym replied, accepting the inevitable at last, 'We must put on a good show for them.'

We walked out to the challenge.

CHAPTER XVII

At the tenth hour of the morning, the bell had rung with huge intention that this was no ordinary combat-by-merit. Most of the audience knew I was damned by my father's actions and then slighted by my cousin, Sir Pym Sans-Brys. The rest there acknowledged that it was honour for me to regain my estate and wished me the best for it.

The first challenge was in archery. Pomphrett Greyrivers presided over this match as Sans-Brys and I made several goes at the target. Most of the results here ended in a stalemate, with our arrows stuck beside one another in the middle circle. *It was apparent we were both well-skilled in this field.* Sans-Brys may have once been a warrior, but I, too, had a hand in it, learning the same as a child *well before* my father's transgression.

The last target, unfortunately, went to Sans-Brys, as he made 'show of it'. He needn't rub it in, of course, yet I feared for the overall outcome. I reckoned his winning the archery would put a small notch in his belt against me. Despite his enmity being no longer the case, the audience did not know of this, so we made sport as best we could.

The next and deciding challenge would be swordsmanship. John Clarence was the referee here. He had us take our places. We nodded to acknowledge one another and began the *duel*. The true determination rested on this and we really had to work at it. I decided to fight hard, showing my cousin he will not get away with the humiliation he put against me. *I so desperately wanted to kill him, deep down... never mind this running off abroad with the woman he loves.*

The round began with Clarence shouting, 'And, go!' A whistle blew in the wind and my cousin and I were locked in our most personal battle ever.

Sword fighting, I felt, was far trickier than archery. When the arrow is fired, fate usually directs its destiny (of course, this is dependent on the archer himself). Not so with a sword, with the opponent directly in front. I tried my best to divert his blows and further advancement upon me. I lunged, he lunged, and I later fell over. Then I regained my composure, carrying on the combat.

Several rounds later, I was already sweating between the layers. Sans-Brys did not blink or show distress, but I bet his body was glistening beneath his layers! We carried on, blow by blow; my mind held focus. I hadn't a chance to glimpse at the many spectators that rallied for my cause. I had noticed that Sans-Brys, with all the nerve, had casually glanced at Cyndosia, who sat in the front row, next to her mother.

No words passed between us, for our swords spoke louder and harsher sentiments. At times, the clash of metal clanging bitterly caused a stinging ring-tone to the ear, which melted away any further desire for mercy...but I had to be merciful to this love-struck soldier. I wondered if his love for dear Cyndosia was truly genuine, indeed. Perhaps it was genuine. He certainly experienced a change of pace since meeting the lovely Matthia. It might have driven him to his senses... *or he lost them upon meeting Cyndosia afterwards.*

I saw an opportunity to end this bitter match once and for all. I lunged my sword into Sans-Brys, into his side, below his rib cage. In reaction, his sword clipped me round the ear, taking some strands of my hair with it. *That would leave a mark, but at least the hair will grow back.*

We both went down and after a few seconds, Clarence announced a draw. A bell was sounded, ending the match. We were a bloody mess and duly removed from the field. Totteringstate Hall was nearby and it was resolved by my friends and a few others to take us there.

Thia stayed with Cateliffe, Nay-Smith and Tudmond, who drove the cart I was in. Sans-Brys was put in a separate cart; Cyndosia and her mother stayed with him. The majority of the crowd remained to witness the other sporting events continuing through into the evening.

Wilf also accompanied me on the return to Totteringstate Hall. He was in the cart with me. It seemed like old times and endless reminiscing held our minds.

'Good thrust, my brother. You could have killed him,' Wilf commented.

'No, I could not kill him. The wound I gave him was not severe enough.' I contemplated telling Wilf about my earlier meeting with Sans-Brys. I looked at him with telling eyes.

'Well, I will be with you,' he paused, noticing my outlook, 'Is there something wrong, Roger?'

I exhaled a breath, 'I've a confession to make, but not officially. Do keep this under your cassock, eh?'

'Oh? What is it? Do tell!'

'Sans-Brys and I made up just before the matches. He plans to travel abroad... there's a girl, who's the daughter of the impresario's godmother. I doubt the cad would make it though, ha-ha. Supposedly, he'd fallen in love and changed his ways.' I could barely speak.

Wilf's eyes widened, 'He could not have changed his ways that much. It looked like he would have enjoyed the kill.'

'That is what we planned. We had to make out that we were still enemies. I had already forgiven him, but told him we had to 'make show of it'.'

'No, you could not let him off that lightly. Not with a paying audience that attends these events all the time. The disappointment could start an internal conflict. We have enough problems. God, so you really made up with the fellow?'

'Yea, I did,' I whispered, and closed my eyes for a quick rest.

Wilf remained on the alert to be certain we would return to Totteringstate safely. The Hall was looming in the distance and a pretty sight for his sore eyes.

'Rog, Rog,' he exclaimed, 'We're nearly there. It's just like old times.'

Weakly I lifted my head to see the outline of the Hall. My heart lifted its dampened spirit and threw it aside, as I held onto my brother.

'Sans-Brys has no further intention of keeping us from our heritage,' I said.

Wilf looked at me, 'That means we've regained Totteringstate for our family!'

'You're still in the clergy house at the Church.'

'Yes, yes, I know. But you and Thia will now have a home. A *proper* home. Not that pigsty of a place you call Hastings Court.'

'I had not built it, remember. Dear William did, just before he planned his home at Totteringstate.'

'Still a shithouse with your shit-stained workforce,' he mocked.

'They are my friends,' I protested, 'And I am deeply fond of them.'

'Will you invite your sty-friends to the Hall?'

'Damn right I will, and I may have them stay over too. There is plenty of room.' I gasped for air.

'Sorry, brother, I did not mean to cause upset.' Wilf tucked the blanket tightly 'round my body. He then asked, 'What's that girl's name, then?'

'Cyndosia Barbellicos.'

'Sounds like someone Sans-Brys would fall for,' Wilf laughed.

I also told Wilf about Matthia. 'That play we saw yesterday...'

'Yes?'

'The actress who played the lead is Thia's cousin, Matthia. Sans-Brys was so worked up to meet this girl and was all in heat about it.'

'Go on,' Wilf eagerly pestered.

'Well,' I smiled, 'It turned out that Matthia was a fellow called Matthias and the look on Pym's face was something to cherish.'

'An egomaniac like him deflated by a curiosity of sex.'

We both laughed. Oddly enough, I was feeling better. 'She did state she 'dressed up' full time and her talent works well in the community.'

'It is not something I would condone, but Heaven bless those who make us happy.'

'That is the way she saw it too,' I added.

'Well, I never,' Wilf pondered.

'You wouldn't want to,' I assured him.

We finally made it to Totteringstate Hall. Sans-Brys and I were put in separate rooms on the ground floor and made as comfortable as possible. The convalescence would take time; with good friends and family, maybe a doctor, it was hoped we would recover soon.

A day or so later, a doctor was called in to see how we were doing. Word had gotten 'round the village by those concerned. A notice of our convalescence was posted at the tavern on Wilset Green. Alexi's troupe had already moved on to the West Counties, to continue their last-leg splendour. It was then arranged for Cyndosia and her mother to make their own way back to Italy from Sydmouth Harbour, hopefully with Sans-Brys in tow. *So much for planning, then!*

Thia and Cyndosia had taken care of Sans-Brys and myself well, but a doctor's word was needed to check progress. A local called Dr Oliviyay had practised medicine for much of his life. He was a middle-aged fellow with a square face, having the look of wisdom in his eyes. He certainly was no unbalanced *humours-and-leeches man*. He had proactive and progressive beliefs. This doctor believed in cleanliness and felt the body relied upon more than just *theories* regarding the elements. He was unhappy with those misguided souls of the profession whose cures usually hurt or caused more problems than they were worth. Old wive's tales might have said much, but the doctor enjoyed proving them otherwise, especially if something better was to be found.

In the early afternoon, Dr Oliviyay rode out to Totteringstate Hall on his trusted horse, Merleron. When he reached the grand estate, he hitched up and went inside. He was met by Cyndosia and Elizabethia.

The doctor announced himself. 'I am Dr Oliviyay and here for service, ladies. Who shall I attend first?'

Cyndosia lunged forward, wild with desperation, 'Please see Pym first. He is getting feverish and his wound is ghastly!'

'Now, now, please calm down,' the doctor soothed, then looking at Thia, asked, 'What about you?'

'Roger is fine,' she stated coolly, unlike Cyndosia, 'I helped clean and redress the wound. I just put a fresh bandage on him before your arrival.'

'Right. I will see to Roger shortly. Let us go to Pym; I would not wish the little lady to worry herself into her grave,' Dr Oliviyay said, as he followed Cyndosia into Pym's room.

Thia accepted this, 'As ye wish. I will make sure Roger is made comfortable for your visit.'

The doctor went into Pym's room, where he was tucked in the bed, but was moaning pretty intensely.

Dr Oliviyay asked Cyndosia, 'How long has he been like this?'

'This morning,' she said, beside herself, 'I tried to help.'

'Hysterics and medicine do not mix, young lady. Keep calm and I can see what I can do here.'

The bandage was checked and it was needing a change, as the blood and ooze was weeping beyond its borders.

'Right,' the doctor ordered Cyndosia, 'I will need fresh water, bandages, and clean linen. I will get my ointments out. I will also need fresh bed sheets. I do not want Pym to remain in this bed as it is.'

Cyndosia ran off to fetch the required items and Oliviyay took out a mixture from his bag. Once the items arrived, Oliviyay went to work, with Cyndosia's assistance.

The doctor got Pym out of bed and removed the bandage he had on, exposing the wound.

'Open the window just a bit, please, dear girl,' the doctor requested.

Cyndosia stopped changing the sheets to open the window. Then, she resumed the bed changing. She took the used linens and threw them in a wall chute in the room.

Dr Oliviyay had examined the wound and cleaned it up. He took his mixture of tree sap and honey and applied it. A fresh bandage had been put around Pym's torso. Pym sighed with relief and it was apparent he felt better.

The bed was clean and ready for Pym to re-enter. Cyndosia helped her love into the bed, tucked him in and kissed him tenderly.

'For when I join thee,' Pym whispered to her, returning her kiss. He looked dreamy and put much of his faith in Cyndosia's love. *She certainly did not disappoint; he had found his Venus.*

'I trust you are better, now. It was just a matter of cleansing and redressing the wound. A bit of fresh air and clean bedding does the rest,' Dr Oliviyay explained.

'No leeches, then?' Pym joked, 'I guess you don't wish to reveal your secrets to me.'

'I do not believe in leech-work. They are most foul and there are better methods of blood letting. In your case, you'd let too much blood. If this took its course, you *would* die from your wound.'

'Sound advice, I guess. You should write a book,' Pym thought aloud.

'I already had, but it is too progressive for some. Maybe time will prove me correct in a couple of hundred years or so,' Oliviyay chuckled, 'Now that you've been sorted, I will go see the other patient.'

The doctor walked out and into my room. I felt lazy and shattered when he entered the room.

I looked up and greeted him, weakly, 'Hello.'

'You look chipper, compared to your compatriot in the other room,' Oliviyay observed.

'I don't feel it, but if you say so,' I exhaled bitterly.

He noticed the bandage around my head, 'Let me see that ear of yours.' He turned my head to see my ear, carefully looked after. 'Nice work, who did it?'

'My wife, Thia,' I revealed.

'Seems she's got composure compared to the other girl. She does not possess the *ugh, that's gross* factor. Very fetching.'

The doctor asked me questions regarding my overall health, which I was positive about and told him so.

'With your respective ladies in attendance to you both, I reckon you will make a good recovery,' Oliviyay stated, 'Good day to you all and don't hesitate to contact me if needed.'

The doctor walked out of the Hall and rode away. One could hear the hooves grow fainter in the distance. Thia gave me a kiss and whispered thanks unto God in my good ear. I smiled and she walked out to see how Pym was doing, now that he was all cleaned up.

Pym was sitting up, resting in bed. 'Elizabethia,' he addressed, 'So, you are helping me, too?'

'I would help anyone in need, Pym,' she answered, walking into the room, 'Even you.'

'Do you forgive me for my past indiscretion upon you?'

'I hadn't given it a second thought. I think you are better off with Cyndosia, anyway.'

Pym smiled, thinking of his plan, 'I want to marry her. You're invited, of course.'

'I would not miss it for the world. At least Rog is on the mend.'

'I am glad to hear it and that our duel ended evenly,' he admitted, 'I had loved you for the wrong reasons.'

My earlier suspicion transferred to her. 'Was there anything between you and Rog before the match?'

'No, love. I just wanted to back out, as I no longer felt the need to scourge him any longer. I got what I wanted and I wanted out.'

'You couldn't do it, though, for many people expected you to fight.'

'I know and I am sorry.' He began to weep. Thia wanted to comfort him, but if Cyndosia walked in, it would look rough indeed. She went to find Pym's love.

Cyndosia was getting a cup of ale when she met Thia outside the rooms.

'I could use one,' Thia jested.

'This one's for Pym.'

'I figured that. I strongly believe he will need it, as he seems distressed.'

Cyndosia's concern grew, 'Why?'

'He was making up with me and it was like talking to melted butter. I had never imagined such a change in a man like him.'

'I guess I was the right person to resolve his issues. I am rich, available and good looking,' she gave a smile.

She walked into Pym's room to give him the ale. He thanked her with a long kiss, and she returned to the corridor resume her conversation with Thia.

'Nothing special about me,' Thia stated, 'I'm just a plain girl with a mattress maker for a father and good spirit all round. I could not imagine what came over Pym to seek me out.'

'That is a man for you. Could be rivalry. After all, our men fought one another.'

'There was more to it than that, but let us leave the matter elsewhere. We have work to do.'

'Yes,' she agreed, peering at Thia closely, 'You know, you and I are so much alike.'

'How so?'

'Appearance… I do not know. I think there may be a connection.'

'That's as far fetched as Roger becoming the King of England,' Thia laughed.

'Well, I do not know, but we may have something.'

'You're a Mediterranean beauty and I am just this English plainsong.'

'You are just as beautiful as me,' Cyndosia argued and gave Thia a hug, 'If you do make it to our wedding, I would like you to be my bridesmaid.'

'Sounds good to me,' Thia smiled, 'However, if we do look alike, just don't put *me* in the wedding gown!'

Cyndosia giggled, 'You English girls are so funny! I loved that play your cousin performed in.'

'Glad to hear that,' Thia wondered if she should reveal Matthia's true identity. *Nah...* she thought not to and sat with Cyndosia in the corridor doing needlework well into the evening hours.

CHAPTER XVIII

Sans-Brys and I had recovered from our respective injuries dealt in the name of honour, now a few weeks hence. Pym had recollected himself mostly from the fresh air outdoors on a lounge chair especially made for him. Cyndosia and her mother stayed with him, yet the mother herself stayed away so the couple could get to know one another. Normally, this would never happen. However, as Pym was in need and the mother and daughter were foreign, intending to take him back as a human souvenir from England, the closeness was allowed. Considering Pym's state, Cyndosia kept her distance in respect to the intimate side of the relationship, just resorting to a fond kiss or cuddle.

The fete was an overall success for the village. Monies collected went toward the village, charity and the Church. Everyone had a good time and that play presented by the Italian players gave many a topic to discuss at *The Wilset Green*.   Last I heard, they toured the West Counties before setting off for the Continent from the Cornish coast. *I reckoned they would be home by now.*

My health was regained rather quickly and I helped around the house, working with Thia and Cyndosia in order to get Pym better. (My other motive, of course, was to remove Pym off these premises permanently so Thia and I could take over, reclaiming the estate.)

My relationship with Pym was far more tranquil than before. We had not crossed swords, by metal or word, since that challenge. He had calmed down considerably and was constantly talking about his wish to marry Cyndosia. It was nice to take him as a family member again, and with some new members about to join in, it was a pity they planned to live abroad. For the sake of Totteringstate Hall, I was willing to go along with this and laboured daily to get him closer toward that goal.

My co-workers at the farm had also been working hard, and when I had told them about the upcoming nuptials, they were most eager to strive further. They knew I wanted Pym out, and were more than happy to support me. Cateliffe and Nay-Smith had bunked out at the Hall to set upon a small patch in the garden to grow various herbs and vegetables. The rest of the workers remained at the farm growing and feeding pigs which will supply some of the food after the ceremony.

We all carried on working toward *something* and Pym remained 'lord of the manor'... *for now.* Since he had gotten a little nicer in personality, I confessed to myself that I would miss the fellow. Yet, my thirst to repossess was much stronger and I just merely wished him well in my heart. It would be interesting to meet him in a few year's time, just to see what influence a different country would have on his temperament.

* * * * * *

When the wedding day arrived, two months later, it would be an elaborate affair. No one even questioned the church-read banns, as *everyone* wanted rid of Sans-Brys. *It was obvious he was not well-liked in the community.* The village knew of Cyndosia and how much he was in love with her. They also knew she would not stick around and was eager to return to her native Italy with him.

The marriage was held at Totteringstate Parish Church and Wilf performed the ceremony. There was a feeling of good relief in the air, as the church was slightly larger compared to St Doublet's. We did not feel like many fish in a small net. I was very excited and my mind was well-secure in its objective of getting back Totteringstate. I was asked to be Pym's best man and Thia had accepted to be Cyndosia's bridesmaid. We happily fulfilled our roles therein.

It was not as private as my wedding, due to many people wanting to see Pym off and fully committed to a new life abroad; (although there were some that would have rather seen him *committed*).

The wedding feast was held at Totteringstate Hall. It was a similar event as my marriage to Thia, as mostly family and close friends were in attendance. Pym was in high spirits and, in my opinion, *acted much out of character*. He was *so* joyful; my senses felt this was too good to be true. But there they were, Pym and his lady, Cyndosia. They looked like a very powerful couple indeed, and if their stations were any greater, such as royalty, they would create a formidable dynasty. As I ate my roast, I shuddered at the thought.

'Roger,' Thia touched my hand, 'You alright?'

'Fine, sweety,' I gave her a pork-flavoured kiss, 'I was just thinking.'

Cateliffe perked up. 'What were you thinking, Rog?'

Eavesdropper! I blushed to relay my earlier thoughts to him without Pym catching wind of them. I silently growled and whispered to Thia what it was and she relayed it to Cateliffe. Thankfully, he had tact and good taste in acknowledging my sentiment.

Cyndosia's mother came up to me to give me a hug. I stood up, wiping my mouth with a cloth, and we embraced. *I would not want to stain her fancy armoury!*

'It is good to be part of your illustrious family,' she said, with a degree of pride.

'Thank you. It is nice to have distant relations, too,' I purred.

Pym got up too, with his bride in tow. 'Roger, we will be leaving in a few days. The ladies and I need to pack and arrange the transport. You can hold off until then, yes?'

'Yea, I can so do. Sydmouth Harbour has ships that travel to the Continent. We will see you off.'

'Much obliged, cousin.' He smiled and felt light-in-heart.

'Bet you cannot wait to consummate,' I giggled.

Pym laughed and, regaining his old attitude, told me, 'Don't be rude, peasant. I do need to keep decorum.'

'As long as you don't keep the decor, you're alright,' I retorted. *Wow, that felt like the old days.*

We parted and I went to rejoin my people. Thia and I embraced and kissed and Tudmond, Tarquinne and Wilset began to play some music. We danced some and I spent private time with Thia looking over my soon-to-be home. I was impressed much of it remained intact, though some bits looked tired and needed minor work. The festivities carried on into the night and there was more to do in order to ensure Pym's departure.

* * * * * *

Pym and Cyndosia spent an extra week at Totteringstate Hall in wedded bliss, despite the presence of the mother-in-law. It was very obvious they were most happy and even more, Pym was planning a new life for himself, by detaching from his former military interests to pursue the intellectual. He had not let on to what he had in mind, but he seemed confident in himself, *without the attitude*.

I remained at Hastings Court with Thia, as we, too, packed for a new life together... at the Hall. We did not have much, as living the peasant life did not carry many effects. *It made the job easier, though.* During that final week we were there, my friends arranged a night at *The Incensed Rose* to wish us farewell. I honestly did not think it should be *final*; after all, I would be a county away from the farm. *Personally, like William, I would not miss the smell.*

We got our drinks and settled down at our usual table upstairs. I sipped my ale and conversations flew freely.

'I can see change in the air,' Cateliffe predicted.

Tarquinne, in his usual homespun humour, began to feel inside his pockets to take out a coin. He piped up, 'Can ye break this large coin for me? I don't seem to have any change.'

Everyone at the table moaned at the bad joke. The coin was put away and we carried on drinking.

Brackbury said, 'We will all miss you, Rog. You will be the lord of Totteringstate for sure.'

Such peasants came with much ignorance.

'No', I protested, 'I am no different than you, and I am merely relocating to my ancestor's residence, which is rightfully mine. Ye trust me on this; it would not make me a lord or something special.'

'I think it does,' Nay-Smith chipped in, 'You will live in that big manor house. Maybe one day, the king of the realm will knight you for something, and you will surely be our lord, just like your ancestors.'

Hey, wait a minute, *this was getting awkward.* I was shocked with what he said, despite the flattery.

'A king,' I exclaimed, 'Why would a king want business with a dumbfuck peasant like me??!'

'Because you are a very special dumbfuck peasant, Roger,' Cateliffe said, 'You worked this farm to supply our products to the Two Counties. You've made a name for yourself, albeit a new name. Well, if any form of royalty does not notice *that*, then they should return from whence they came.'

'And so shall it be with us,' I stated.

'Eh?' Cateliffe was bemused.

'We should return from whence we came because some of us came from that section of France that conquered this kingdom,' I clarified.

A silence befell our space. I blushed violently, thinking about my friend's thoughts about me. Thia gave me a kiss for comfort.

'Awh, not that again,' Wilset whinged.

'At least they are married this time,' Buckingham spouted and smiled at Thia and I.

'Well, whatever it is,' Cateliffe began a toast, 'Long life and long lasting of the newly formed House of Woodes-Hastings.'

Everyone stood up to partake and I could not stop blushing. I blushed a hue of deep red, *redder than a Crusades battlefield.*

'Rog, angel,' Thia held me.

I turned to her, 'Yes?'

'Your friends really care for you. Their home will be two short soon and already, they are feeling the pain and a hole of loss.'

Perhaps they were; I had to figure out how to compromise my new status and keep the relationship with my friends stable. I soon realised a possibility...

I stood up to announce, 'I understand you all feel for me and wish me the best. I know you will all miss me deeply as a friend and fellow worker. It is not as if I am the one going abroad. I will be a county away and plan to run the farm from there. I could do the accounting and come out to work with you like I did before.'

I sat down, awaiting their response. It was apparent that Wilset's *candle-in-the-mind* had dimmed slightly.

He asked, 'So you are not leaving us after all?'

Everyone stared; Tudmond spoke quietly to Wilset. 'He is only living at Totteringstate. He just said he will be with us. He is not going to the moon or the Continent, like Sans-Brys. We will work as we did in the past...maybe just one short on occasion.'

Wilset tended to get overemotional when things got too rough for him. *He would surely sucketh as a warrior, the milksop!*

Our group started separate conversations. I sipped my ale when Buckingham came over to me.

'Rog, I've been thinking,' he began.

'Yea, does it hurt?'

Buckingham sighed at my bad joke and continued, 'No, please listen. I want to help with the accounts, like I did before.'

'You can bring the books over to me and I can check them over and pay your wages and all that.'

'So you *will* be our lord?'

I stared at Buckingham, 'Oh, shut up... I cannot be a lord!'

'Give it up, Rog, you are far better than us. Your lineage is superior and if it weren't for your father, you would have been our lord anyway.'

'*Your* lord?' I smirked.

'Well, maybe in name anyway. You are still one of us, despite what the others think of you,' Buckingham added.

I knew very well what the others thought of me. The sentiment was presented in the statements of Nay-Smith, Wilset, Cateliffe and Buckingham. I did not know how much I could go on like this. I sighed and Thia sat there, holding my hand.

'Once we get rid of that Sans-Brys fellow, we will install you as our lord anyway,' Cateliffe offered.

I was chuffed at this; their kind hearts showed deep seated loyalty, *but the dumbfuck intelligence was getting to me.*

'I do appreciate your honourable intention and I can see you want me to be your *leader*,' I went on, 'As I said. I will be with you *when needed*.'

'That means all the time, right?' Tudmond tried to sound optimistic, 'If not, what do you plan to do with the rest of your time away, Rog?'

I recalled the plant patches Cateliffe and Nay-Smith grew during our convalescence. 'How about I grow my own? There is plenty of space.'

Tudmond laughed, 'Grow your own, he said. What d'you intend to grow?'

Brackbury was more thoughtful, 'I would not knock it. We can add vegetation to our products and sell them at the market. Meat and vegetation... a complete meal at reasonable cost. Could be a winner.'

'Hey, that's right,' Nay-Smith quipped, 'We can also add this to our pig feeds.'

'Well, Roger, your usefulness will continue to be essential to our work,' Cateliffe remarked.

I guess the destiny of the grand Hall will prove most convenient...

* * * * * *

A few days later, Sydmouth Harbour was bustling with activity with ships waiting for passengers to board them, with Sans-Brys and his party amongst the crowd. A barge, bound for the Continent, had been readied and people began to board her. Thia and I went to Pym and his family to bid them farewell. My friends stayed behind at the farm, for obvious reasons.

Cyndosia's mother was pleased we turned up at their send-off. She gave me a hug and said tearfully, 'It was very nice to meet you and thank you for everything.'

"'Twas no matter, ma'am,' I said.

Cyndosia and Thia also said their goodbyes, 'I will miss you,' Cyndosia lamented, 'I wish we gotten to know one another better.'

Thia was sad, but tactful, 'We did as expected, under the circumstances.'

'Yes, and got our men healthy again.'

'Aye. You take care of Pym. He deserves a girl like you.'

Thia gave her one final embrace and walked away to find me. I then saw Pym, dressed in nothing less than his flashy self (*as if he could help it*).

He turned to me, 'Roger,' he cried, hugging me in a crushing motion, 'Roger, how can I thank you enough? There is no time of day that can allow me such a course.'

That was odd. He talked like a man in love and men in love say silly things. I was more practical... *it seemed, at least, I'd put him in his place.*

'No need to over do it, Pym,' I pardoned, 'We are now even. Your help at the Hall is thanks enough.'

'Good,' he spoke calmly and the dreamy look was still in his eye.

'What are your plans when you arrive?'

'I cannot predict, Roger, but I will pursue my endeavours the way I pursued you to the sword.'

Now *THAT* sounded more like the man I once knew.

'I wish you well and good luck in your pursuits. Take care of your family,' I shook his hand.

'I will and you do likewise. Give Thia a kiss for me, eh?'

Yep, it was Pym all right!

'I will,' I said, walking away to give him room to board. I noticed the passengers were swelling into the ship and Sans-Brys and his family disappearing amongst them.

'Well, Thia, that is it. This is what we've been waiting for, for a long time,' I exhaled, pondering ideas about for the Hall.

'Let's not think on it,' Thia persuaded, 'We can now move on, as they will.'

Cateliffe discreetly worked his way through the crowd to find us. He had a horse and cart waiting to take Thia and I home... *our real home in Totteringstate*. We got into the cart and Cateliffe navigated the horse away from the Harbour. Most of the well-wishers had dispersed, as the ship was moving out of its dock. I sighed heavily, seeing the passengers aboard waving wildly at their loved ones on shore. I caught sight of Pym who waved and nodded at me. I returned the wave. He looked at Cyndosia and walked away from the ship's edge toward the middle of the deck. I was most happy for him, *but more relieved at getting our home back.*

About two months later, Thia and I were settled in Totteringstate. She was with child, too. At last, we had a family in the making. It was such a relief to finally spread our wings, as our activity was rather limited at Hastings Court. Luckily, we did not have much work to do at the Hall itself, either.

We bought some new furniture and gave some of the more tired-looking pieces to our friends at the Court, as a thank you, for which they were most grateful. *It made them feel more than what they were.* Despite my lack of love for Sans-Brys, at least he respected the property and we were most pleased to see it come to shape with the Woodes-Hastings touch. *The outer edges needed work, however...*

A letter arrived on our doorstep one day. Thia walked through the corridor to pick it up. On the face of it, one can see very exquisite handwriting. She noted it was obvious Pym had kept to his intent on bettering himself. As it was addressed to me, she went into one of the ground floor rooms I used as a study.

She looked at me as I carefully opened it, breaking its blue seal. It read:

Dear Roger,

We made it past the Channel on a fair wind and calm seas. As it was impractical to go to Italy strictly by water, we landed in France and took horse south-easterly. We stayed with Cyndosia's mother for a spell before buying our own place which looks out to sea. Cyndosia is already with child and preparing for the event alongside her mother. The two of them cannot stop cackling!

As for my intellectual pursuits, I discovered there was a local university seeking a Professor of Arts. When I applied in person, I gained the professorship straight away as they saw in my person the most perfect and beautiful specimen they ever saw in their lives. These Italians thought I looked like one of their gods of ancient times, brought back to life. They wished me upon this pedestal as a life model, in addition to the lectures I would give. The course included all-male students and they paid me very well for it. It sounded like a good direction to take and I did not disappoint.

Anyhow, I left your precious Totteringstate in good condition, as you would like it. I respected and kept it up for you, as I was told to do initially. I predicted someday you would return and reclaim it for your own.

Give my love to Thia and best wishes to ye all.

Your Cousin, Pym Sans-Brys

I was pleased to hear he made a new home for himself and as for his appointment as a life model, I could not comment. I wondered about it, but let it go. It certainly appealed to his insane vanity and he could keep up the lifestyle Cyndosia was accustomed to.

I shared the letter with Thia, who laughed at the model reference.

'This is nude modelling, I believe,' she giggled.

'Oh, tish,' I dismissed.

'It must be; you remember how the players were like. Italians are into this sort of thing. What else would one think?'

'I don't know, but I would rather not,' I stated.

But I knew she had a point there. If this got back to my friends in Dumfushire, the gossip would rage like wildfire between the Two Counties and the ridicule it would continually generate. *This was a family matter; it was no one else's business.*

I picked up the letter again to re-read it, then threw it into the active fireplace.

Thia cried, 'Rog, what did you do that for?'

'To keep the peace. I saw your reaction. Imagine our friends' reactions. Leave Pym to his dignity on these shores and let him be naked elsewhere in silence.'

'Sound words, love,' she kissed me, 'Your friends definitely were right about you being special.'

Well, I thought it was the right thing to do. *If I were of my original station in life, this would have been expected.*

CHAPTER XIX

Some years had passed and it was early in the new decade of the 1290s. Much has happened since the departure of Sans-Brys, who by now became a distant memory. Occasionally, we had a laugh about him within the familial circle, but I kept my personal vow regarding his newfound lifestyle. I never told my friends at Dumfushire; I felt Sans-Brys deserved better, *even though I felt otherwise.*

My family had grown considerably; our domiciliation at Totteringstate thus became a necessity. Thia bore me eight children, but only three survived: Alexander Edward, aged twelve; Roger Henry, aged ten and my most precious, Dorothia Jane, aged seven. I needn't go into detail about the losses, as it broke my heart at the time and had become a scathing recollection for me. However, three could do wonders and they were as solid and sturdy as all my farming friends combined... *but the children made far better company.* They filled the Hall with delight and it was a real blessing to see them growing up. Thia and I continued to be intimate and discovered ways to get close that gave no consequence. I loved her as a faithful servant through our time together.

The farm thrived well under the tutelage of Buckingham, Cateliffe, Nay-Smith, Tudmond, Wilset, and the rest. They hired new hands on and off for a spell during the busier periods. As our farm got more productive, word got out and our reputation spread. Some orders came from far distances, so we shipped them out live in those cases and let receivers do the work. Popularity for our meat spread beyond the Two Counties and got as far as the higher orders of the land.

I got a letter the other day which astounded me. It apparently looked of regal origin and the seal shown symbols of Royal authority. *I was stunned that anyone of Royal circles would single me out for a sent message.* I opened the letter, written in the most exquisite hand and read:

Edward Plantagenet, King of England

Roger Alexander Woodes-Hastings

It is with great pleasure to notify you of a progress I am to undertake. My courtiers suggested I visit Dumfushire, wherefrom they sampled excellent meats in the local area at a previous time. I had heard of a large estate of land in Woolanshire, which includes a house called Totteringstate Hall, and consider it fit to make camp for my party.

Edward Plantagenet

I ran to Thia with the news and saddled a horse to ride out to Dumfushire to inform my workers at the farm. They laboured hard as ever to get as many pigs ready for the event.

For weeks, we prepared for the Royal visit. Cateliffe and Nay-Smith stayed with me at the Hall to prepare the estate and act as my *servants*. Eventually, the King's tour had progressed into our locality. When He did arrive, it was nothing but splendour. He had a court of many, as all Kings did. *They would bring everything, even the kitchen basin!*

He had the best finery that could be smelted from the earth. He was well built, roughly over six foot tall with long legs and arms, which kept his horse secured during His travels. His complexion looked dark and his personality housed a temper that no pot could out-boil. This was *The King*... The King who left a border of crenellation in the West, hammered the North, and expulsed the foreigner. He looked commanding atop his horse which was laden with decorations of his livelihood... *his coat of arms*. He passed through many shit stained roads and city streets without a mark on him. It was because He was *The King* and it was a capital offence to even wish such a mark upon Him.

I was riding my horse to scan the area for the King's party. I went as far as the toll bridge, near the monastery (where the Progress spent a night). A horse in the train had stumbled over a loose rock near the bridge and one of the Party had fallen in the river. *It was obvious that he could not swim.* The horse fell upon him, nearly setting him to drown. I jumped in and saved him; *my early days spent swimming in the river had paid off.* He was wearing very fanciful gear and it was a rather cursèd struggle. I was getting tangled amongst his fine pieces, *but these pieces were worthless in the mouth of a river!*

The horse sorted itself out and walked ashore, shaking itself off. As I pulled him out, the man said to me that he lost a special brooch and could I retrieve it for him. *I thought better of it, but did him the service anyway.* I plunged into the river, for I knew it was only about three foot deep and a shiny object could be seen, *if one knew where to look.* I raced in my search and found it beside an underwater plant. There it stood, like the Northern Star, but with an opposing, circular shape. It looked most precious and probably worth well beyond our wage-packets combined. I rose from the water and gave it to him and smiled.

'Took a bit to find such an item, but here 'tis, my lord,' I replied. *He must be some lord, being within the Progress.*

'I so deeply thank you, kind one. This item has deep meaning for me and it is good that you found it,' the grateful man answered, sodden in his beautiful velvet and fur clothing and woollen cloak.

My cheeks began to go red. The weather was not too cold today, so I suggested the man remove his cloak and other wet apparel for the time being. An underling, riding at the back of the long queue of horses, ran to give the man his own cloak, where the brooch was reattached. A space in a cart was made for the downed man.

The King approached. I knelt immediately and addressed him.

'Your Majesty.'

'Your bravery and knowledge of the river was well noted today,' the King commended, 'You rescued my favourite adviser, Lord Simon DeMontasqueue', as well as that brooch I gave to him on his last birthday. Sardin' thing cost me a fortune, that did!'

I looked up to see the most intensive eyes I had ever seen.

The King continued, 'And you are?'

'Roger Alexander Woodes-Hastings of Totteringstate, descended from William Phillip de Hastings of Sur-Le-Merde, France.'

'Ah yes, the pig farmers! My courtiers told me all about your tasty meats, yum-yum,' He winked and licked his lips.

My mind drew a blank; the savage blush returned to my cheeks.

'Aye, I am a pig farmer, Your Majesty,' I answered Him.

The King asked for His sword... *His best, decorative sword.*

'Roger Alexander Woodes-Hastings, by the power vested in me, Edward Plantagenet, King of England, knight thee, Sir Roger Alexander Woodes-Hastings, Lord of Totteringstate.'

Holy shit, I got knighted... and reinstated into the aristocracy. My heart leaped for joy... *the curse was no longer upon me.*

The King smiled, 'Alright?'

'Yea,' I smiled back.

He said impatiently, 'Let's get a move on, I haven't the time of day and I am quite famished. We will banquet at your Hall and make camp as I requested. Prepare for me one of your rooms, I do not wish to camp with the rest of the clods,' the King signalled and rode off.

I mounted my trusty horse and raced it to Totteringstate. I had to get there *before* the King and his entourage.

I reached the Hall itself and continued in my haste to see my beloved Thia.

She was waiting by the front window as I barged in, catching her unaware.

I cried, 'Guess what?'

Thia looked at me, 'What?' She then looked at my condition, 'Oh Rog, you're all wet!'

'Never mind that, The King is coming.'

With disbelief, she remarked flippantly, 'Yea, and I'm the Lady Thia of the Dumfushire Stone.'

I laughed at her crack'd joke, but got serious, 'Silly lass, I just got knighted!'

'WHAT?' She nearly fainted.

'You are truly a Lady, now,' I purred into her ear and we kissed in a fleeting divinity, 'I will explain later. I've got to change quickly. Come and help me.'

We went into our bedroom, where we set a brutal raid upon the wardrobe to find proper apparel... *well, as primrose clean as one could get, given the times.*

The Progress moved slowly down the path, getting closer to Totteringstate Hall. I gathered Thia and the children, as well as Cateliffe and Nay-Smith to receive the King. It was the most exciting moment of our lives...

...and, at last, our little Woodes-Hastings dynasty had begun.

www.ingramcontent.com/pod-product-compliance
Lightning Source LLC
Chambersburg PA
CBHW021017120726
47905CB00009B/3052